Monday, May 11, 1953

The richest homosexual in San Francisco is a private investigator.

Nick Williams lives in a modest bungalow with his fireman husband, a sweet fellow from Georgia by the name of Carter Jones.

Nick's gem of a secretary, Marnie Wilson, is worried that Nick isn't working enough. She knits a lot.

Jeffery Klein, Esquire, is Nick's friend and lawyer. He represents the guys and gals who get caught in police raids in the Tenderloin.

Lt. Mike Robertson is Nick's first love and best friend. He's a good guy who's one hell of a cop.

The Unexpected Heiress is where their stories begin. Read along and fall in love with the City where cable cars climb halfway to the stars.

The Unexpected Heiress

Nick Williams Mysteries

The Unexpected Heiress
The Amorous Attorney
The Sartorial Senator
The Laconic Lumberjack
The Perplexed Pumpkin
The Savage Son
The Mangled Mobster
The Iniquitous Investigator
The Voluptuous Vixen
The Timid Traitor
The Sodden Sailor
The Excluded Exile
The Paradoxical Parent
The Pitiful Player
The Childish Churl

The Rotten Rancher

A Happy Holiday

The Adroit Alien

The Leaping Lord

The Constant Caprese

The Shameless Sodomite

The Harried Husband

The Stymied Star

The Roving Refugee

The Perfidious Parolee

Nick & Carter Stories

An Enchanted Beginning

Golden Gate Love Stories

The One He Waited For

Their Own Hidden Island

Daytona Beach Stories

The Sailor Who Washed Ashore

The Unexpected Heiress

A Nick Williams Mystery
Book 1
By Frank W. Butterfield

Published With Delight
By The Author
MMXVII

The Unexpected Heiress

Copyright © 2017 by Frank W. Butterfield.

All rights reserved.

ISBN-10: 1544618840
ISBN-13: 978-1544618845

First publication: June 2016
Second edition: December 2016
Third edition: March 2017

No part of this book shall be reproduced, stored in a retrieval system, or transmitted by any means–electronic, mechanical, photocopying, recording, or otherwise–without written permission from the publisher.

Brief excerpts for the purpose of review are permitted.

This book contains explicit language and suggestive situations.

This is a work of fiction that refers to historical figures, locales, and events, along with many completely fictional ones. The primary characters are utterly fictional and do not resemble anyone that I have ever met or known of.

Be the first to know about new releases:

frankwbutterfield.com

NW01-B-20190212

Contents

Author's Introduction..1

Chapter 1...5

Chapter 2...11

Chapter 3...19

Chapter 4...27

Chapter 5...35

Chapter 6...41

Chapter 7...47

Chapter 8...55

Chapter 9...63

Chapter 10...71

Chapter 11...79

Chapter 12...85

Chapter 13..89

Chapter 14..95

Chapter 15..103

Chapter 16..111

Chapter 17..121

Chapter 18..131

Chapter 19..139

Author's Note...147

Acknowledgments..................................149

Historical Notes.......................................151

Credits...155

More Information....................................157

To all our queer, odd, and strange ancestors who made it possible to live modern lives of so much freedom.

Thank you.

Unexpected

\ən-ik-ˈspek-təd\

1. Not expected. Unforeseen.

Heiress

\ˈer-əs\

1. A woman who is an heir especially to great wealth.

Author's Introduction

Daytona Beach, Fla.
September 16, 2017
A few minutes past 1 in the afternoon

Thanks for your interest in *The Unexpected Heiress*!

This is the first book in what is now a series of fourteen volumes with three additional books on the side. When I first sat down to write this story, I had no idea what I was getting myself into. But I'm awfully glad that I did. What a fun ride it's been!

I had no idea where this story was going beyond the first chapter, but I let the story write itself and let the characters introduce themselves. That's still the way it works and it makes writing these stories a whole heck of a lot of fun.

Without giving too much away, I can tell you there are six people you'll meet in this book who will, if you'll let them, be revealing more and more of themselves to you as the stories continue from one book to the next.

First, there's Nick. He's the narrator. He grew up in what he calls a "big pile of rocks" on Nob Hill in San Francisco, mostly during the Depression. He lives in Eureka Valley (you probably know it as The Castro) and drives around town in a 1952 Buick Super. He's been a private dick for a few years. Before that, he was an orderly at the City Hospital down on Potrero. And before that, he was a medical corpsman in the Navy, back during the war.

Then, there's Marnie. She's Nick's secretary and a great gal. Nick works, but he's not too busy, so she's taught herself to knit since she started working for him back in 1950.

Next is Jeffery. He's a lawyer whose swank office is on the tenth floor of the Shell Building down at the bottom of Bush Street. He's Nick's lawyer, his friend, and was once his lover.

And then there's Carter. He's the love of Nick's life and they live together in a little bungalow on Hartford Street. He's a big guy. Stands at 6'4" and, as a devotee of physical culture, is covered with muscles. He's a fireman down at Station 3 on Post Street. Or he was. But lately he's been off work because of an unfortunate run-in with a fire truck. He's from Georgia and first came to San Francisco back in '39.

Next, we have Mike. He's a big guy, too. A little taller than Carter. He has electric blue eyes along with a face that someone once called, "movie monster handsome." He's a police lieutenant at the North District station and a real good guy all around. He was Nick's first lover and is still his best friend.

Finally, we have Dr. Williams, Nick's father. He's something else. I'll let him introduce himself to you. That's probably best.

In *The Unexpected Heiress*, you get to meet these folks

and decide if you like them well enough to know more about them. If you do, I hope you'll move on to *The Amorous Attorney*, which takes us down Mexico way and involves... I don't wanna give too much away. Not yet.

Well, that's it. I'll let Nick take over from here. Have a walk around. Kick the tires. See how it goes. Enjoy your time with Nick, Carter, Marnie, Mike, and the rest of the gang. And be sure to let me know what you think: frankwbutterfield.com

Chapter 1

777 Bush Street, Third Floor
San Francisco, Cal.
Monday, May 11, 1953
Half past 10 in the morning

She walked through the door of my private office like she was gliding on air.

Her curves were definitely in all the right places. The dress she wore made sure I knew it.

She removed the veil from her face and pinned it back on her hat, which was perched precariously on her upswept hair.

She sat down and leaned in, making sure I could see all the way down her ample cleavage.

As she sat there, I asked, "Would you like a cigarette?"

She smiled and nodded. I offered her one and she took it. I leaned over and lit it for her.

She pulled on it like she was finally getting a drink of

water after a forced march in the desert. When she exhaled, she smiled at me and asked, "You work alone?"

I nodded. "How can I help?"

She looked down demurely as if there was one very specific way I could help.

I waited.

Finally, she looked up and said, "It's over between me and Johnny and I need some proof."

I took out a pad and pencil and began to make some notes. We went through the usual questions: her name, his name, how long they'd been married, her address, the hotel she thought he had been habituating of late, and, most importantly, the name of the other woman.

"Oh, but Mr. Williams, it ain't some dame, it's a guy." She spit out the last words like she'd just bit down on a sour pickle and couldn't wait to be rid of it.

I looked up and said, "Yeah?"

She nodded. "If I'd known Johnny was a fairy when I married him..." She looked up and shrugged.

"What? What would you have done?" I asked, keeping my voice level.

"You know. I would have told my pops and he would have had some of the guys down at his bar do a number on Johnny and let him know what's what."

I stood up and put on my coat.

She made an "O" with her mouth. I guessed that was her way of expressing shock or maybe astonishment.

"Wait. How much do I owe you?"

"Not a thin dime, miss."

"Really? You work for free?"

"Oh no," I said as I put on my hat and extended my hand to help her stand up. "I don't work for free."

"I'm confused."

"No, you're not. You're just angry. You thought he

loved you but you knew all along he wasn't the right man. Why did you even marry him?"

Now she was angry. She refused my hand and stayed planted in the chair.

"I had to get out of Pop's house, didn't I?"

"Well, they have wonderful residential hotels for women these days. Or so I'm told. You get three squares, a comfortable bed, and bath down the hall all at an affordable price. Daily, weekly or monthly rates offered."

She giggled. "You're funny."

"No miss. What I am is a homosexual and I don't work for clients who aren't polite and can't even talk about their soon-to-be ex-husbands without calling them words like 'fairy' or 'fruit'."

She stood up haughtily. "I should have known you was one of them. There oughta be a law."

"There is one in most states of our great nation. Now, can I walk you to the elevator while I give you a couple of names to call on? These are gentlemen who will be happy to help you. And they won't care what you call your husband as long as you pay up front and cover their daily incidentals."

She stopped at the door and turned on me. "So, what you're sayin' is that since I called Johnny a fairy, you ain't gonna help me?"

"That's right, miss."

"Well, I never!"

"Well, now you have."

We walked into the front office. I saw Marnie shaking her head as I opened the door.

I walked her down the dark, little hallway to the ancient, creaky elevator and gave her the names of some of the cheaper, but still good enough, private detectives I knew who would gladly help her out.

As the door closed, I lifted my hat and heard her giggle.

I walked back to my office and looked at the letters that had been recently been painted on the frosted glass:

Nicholas Williams
Private Detective
Licensed and Bonded
PR-7777
10 a.m. - 4:30 p.m.
And By Appointment

I sighed and thought about all the money I'd spent to get this office, hire Marnie, get that particular phone number, and even have the glass painted.

Not that it really mattered. I didn't need to work. I had what my friend and attorney Jeffery Klein called, "An unbreakable trust." It was left to me by a venerable great-uncle who, from all accounts, put the word "gay" in the "Gay Nineties" that San Francisco was infamous for.

He was a rake of the worst sort and, apparently, saw the tendency in me, and so skipped everyone else and their outstretched hands and landed the whole pile in my lap at the tender age of 21.

I was surprised and shocked by the bequest. I'd only met old Uncle Paul once, but, as I later learned, he'd been keeping a watchful eye on me through the stormy years of my misspent youth before I'd enlisted in the Navy and gone off to fight for freedom, democracy, and the American Way.

My shock turned to unsurprised disgust when every relative, near and far, decided to sue. The California dockets were cluttered for about five years with the details of Uncle Paul's sordid life and the injustice of handing untold millions over to a kid of 21.

Learned judges rebuked Uncle Paul in writing, and at great length, for his lascivious ways. They lectured me about squandering my inheritance in similar fashion. But, in the end, they had all thrown up their hands and declared the trust was valid and the inheritance was mine to do with as I wanted.

When the whole gang of relatives got together and appealed to the California State Supreme Court, the case was thrown back at them, with a vengeance, and they were told to go home and nurse their wounds.

And they did. None of them, my own father included, would now talk to me and, from what I'd heard, my name was never mentioned on Nob Hill or even down in Hillsborough where some of the younger family members were relocating to build their mansions on vast, two-acre spreads.

I opened the door and saw Marnie standing there, hands on her hips. "So, you threw another one out, didn't you?"

I took off my hat and said, "Don't harass me, Marnie. You know I don't need the work."

"Yeah, I know. You don't need the work. But you go a little stir when you ain't got the work and I love working here.

"Oh! The characters that come through that door give Mother and me a chuckle. It's better than anything on the radio or the TV.

"But, lord! I can't sit here, knitting my hands till they bleed, and watch you slowly go crazy."

I smiled at her and said, "You're a real friend, Marnie."

"Well, I ain't the only one you got. That Klein, he wants to talk to you. Seems like he's got a case for you.

And it's the Polk Street kind."

I put my hat back on my head, gave Marnie a quick kiss on the cheek, and said, "Thanks doll. See you later."

Chapter 2

On Bush Street
Monday, May 11, 1953
A little past 11 in the morning

Jeffery Klein, Esquire, had offices down the street and in another world. His suite was found on the tenth floor of The Shell Building at 100 Bush Street, right at the corner of Battery Street, just a block from Market.

I took a walk down the long, sloping hill. It was only seven blocks but what a difference those seven blocks could make.

The trashy Tenderloin slowly transformed into the more respectable Financial District.

I lit a Camel, not so usual for me those days, as I walked down and passed by building after building of apartments, with some respectable and low-cost hotels, and a flop or two. I strolled past the late-night market and over the Stockton Street Tunnel. The Pacific Telephone Building, a couple of blocks down, now less sloping, from Stockton was right about where the Tenderloin faded away and the Financial District began to assert itself. Three more blocks down on the flat part of Bush, after crossing Montgomery and Sansome, was the glorious Shell Building, all white and gold pushing 29 stories into the sky.

I pushed through its understated but always-shiny brass doors and entered the plush environs of all that 1929 hoped it would become but never quite achieved. Fortunately, even in a depression, the world still ran on oil, so the primary tenant, one Royal Dutch Shell, didn't worry so much about leasing conditions.

The Shell Building was air conditioned, of course, even though no one needed air conditioning when we had the Golden Gate to keep us cool most days. It could be baking over in Sacramento in the middle of July while we were sitting cool in the low 60s. It's why I loved the City. Well, one of the reasons.

Tony, the elevator man, was polite as always. "Welcome back, Mr. Williams."

"How are you today, Tony?"

"Can't complain."

He closed the door and moved the lever to the mark for the tenth floor. I'd been coming in and out of Jeffery's office long enough that he knew me by now.

"How's Anna?"

"She's getting better. Doctor says she may be able to start walking soon."

Anna was the youngest of Tony and Antoinette's four children and the one to catch the polio. It had been a heartbreaking story that involved an iron lung at one point but things were looking up.

"Well, give my best to Antoinette and all the kids and I'll be sending along a little something to help Anna keep her mind off her troubles."

We reached the tenth floor and Tony said, "You're such a kind man, Mr. Williams. I'm sure she'll be happy to have it."

I lifted my hat to him and said, "Have a good day, Tony."

"The same to you, sir." And, with that, the door closed and I turned to the right.

Jeffery's suite of offices was at the end of the hallway. He had the whole side of this building. He'd started his practice right out of the war, in 1945, and specialized in helping any veteran who would come his way, often deferring or refusing payment when he knew the poor guy couldn't afford it. Some of those veterans had done very well for themselves and had brought Jeffery with them as their little enterprises turned into big enterprises. The confidence Jeffery had shown them when he was a one-man outfit in a dusty office had been repaid many times over when these clients had stuck with him. So, instead of moving their business to the white-shoe crowd, as they grew and grew, they stuck with their buddy. It was a real help because, with a last name like Klein, Jeffery would never be in the country-club set, where all the high-flying deals were made, not even in San Francisco.

I opened the door and was greeted by Robert, the cute and all-smiles receptionist. He smiled broadly and said, "Good afternoon, Mr. Williams. I'll let Mr. Klein know you're here. Have a seat, won't you?"

I nodded, took off my hat, and had a seat. I picked up the latest copy of *Time* magazine. There was a nice illustrated photo of the new Secretary of Health, Education, and Welfare on the cover. Eisenhower was settling in, and Oleta Culp Hobby was one of the new ones he was bringing into his cabinet, replacing the old brain trust guys and gals.

I flipped through the magazine and skipped the latest news from Washington and elsewhere, the story detailing the infiltration of Communists in south-east Asia, and turned straight to where the more salacious parts of the magazine are to be found, which are always in the back. A one-paragraph item under "Jots & Notes" caught my eye.

Whither Wells?

> Hollywood boy wonder up for new part in *It Was Raining Then* against vivacious leading lady, his gal pal. Could this mean wedding bells at long last for confirmed bachelor Taylor Wells? Wells and long-time friend, Miss Rhonda Starling, were spotted canoodling at the Copa while in town for contract talks with Metro. No one knows what these two are up to, not even Winchell.

I looked at the picture of Taylor and Rhonda and I knew what they were up to. She was providing cover for him, and he was providing cover for her.

If they got married, it would be strictly for the gifts and the publicity. Her wild parties with the sweater set in Brentwood were getting harder and harder to keep out of the press, or so I'd heard. And his bachelor pad, where no woman had ever been seen, reportedly had a sling in the back bedroom. These tidbits of Hollywood gossip always seemed to float up the coast but no one had ever seen the sling, as far as I could find out.

If Walter Winchell were to find out and publish all the sordid details, or even just a whisper of the truth, in his mean-spirited daily column, that would mean curtains for both Taylor and Rhonda, poor kids.

"Nick!"

I looked up to see Jeffery standing there, perfectly turned out, looking tan, fit, and happy.

I stood up and shook my friend's hand. He always lingered a little longer than most men, but we had our history, and that was OK by me.

I followed him down the thickly carpeted hallway past the artistic touches he'd had put on the walls and into the vast cavern in the sky that was his office.

The window behind his desk was panoramic, to say the least. The Ferry Building, showing the time to be right at 11:30, was on the right. The Golden Gate Bridge was on the left. And all the glorious bay, with Alcatraz in the middle, was in between.

I took my usual seat as Jeffery swept around his desk and took his.

"So, how you been, Nick?"

"Just peachy, Jeffery. And you?"

"Can't complain."

"But you will."

He laughed and said, "OK. So here's the story. Big raid at the Kit Kat on Polk Street last night. Cops picked up about 20 and showed them off to the papers, but mostly the *Examiner*."

I shook my head in disgust.

Jeffery said, "I know. Perversion sells. Particularly in this town."

"And particularly on the front page of the *Examiner*."

"Exactly."

"So, which one of the 20 is your client?"

"That's where it gets interesting. My client managed not to land in the paper. He's the twenty-first, you might say."

"Did they book him?"

"For loitering."

I raised my eyebrows. "Really? Who does he know?"

"Good question. That's one of the first things I want you to find out."

"Why don't you ask your client?"

"I would, but he's down in Hollywood."

I shook my head. "Oh no. I'm not going to play interference for any studio or star."

Jeffery looked at me. "This one is different."

"They're all different. Jeffery. This one can't come to terms because Daddy will disinherit. This one has a morals clause in his contract. That one is married with two kids in school and one on the way. But they're all the same. They're all hiding from themselves."

Jeffery nodded quietly. I came down off my high horse.

"Not everyone has an unbreakable trust like you, Nick."

"I know." I sighed and gave in to the inevitable. "OK. Who is it?"

"Taylor Wells."

I laughed. "Gee, and I just read a little blind item in *Time* about him and Rhonda at the Copa last week. Not even Winchell knows."

Jeffery smiled. "Winchell knows but cash talks and he's not publishing. Part of our job is to make sure he doesn't publish. And your first assignment is to find out who is covering for him inside the police department. We need to know who our friend is."

"Working inside the system this time?"

"I've done it before."

"But not well. I'll keep your name out of it."

"Keep Taylor's out of it too."

"Taylor is it?"

Jeffery just smiled at me.

I stood up. "I assume there is a hefty fee involved?"

"Of course. Metro is picking up all the expenses."

"Well, bully for Metro."

"Write the check to the usual place?"

"You got it. The San Francisco Fireman's Benevolent Fund."

As I turned to leave, Jeffery asked, "How is Carter these days?"

I put my hand on the doorknob and turned to get one last look at the orange span and blue waters off in the distance. "He's doing good. Getting around better. We have our good days and our bad days, just like any married couple."

"He working yet?"

"Not yet. Doing a little arson investigating on the side for the police. He can use his cane to hobble around. He helps them out and they give him good, useful work to do. Keeps him from going crazy."

"Well, give him my love."

"I will. And I'll be in touch."

With that, I shut the door behind me and whistled a show tune as I walked down the hallway. When I rounded the reception desk, I put on my hat.

Robert said, "I just love Mary Martin." I nodded, walked out the door, and kept whistling, all the way to the elevator.

Chapter 3

The Shell Building
100 Bush Street
Monday, May 11, 1953
Just before noon

I picked up a copy of the *Examiner* at the lobby newsstand. Sure enough, there on page one screamed the headline, "Homo Nest Raided. 20 Arrested For Lewdness." The article continued about the brave boys of the North District and how they took on the queers of Polk Gulch at the infamous Kit Kat Club ("One of the denizens told this reporter of a 'marriage' between a femme and her bulldagger. Jake, no last name, was the best man and the maid of honor. No further information is available on how this transformation was achieved.").

There were four newspapers in town: the *Examiner*, the *News*, the *Call-Bulletin*, and the *Chronicle*. The rivalry for subscribers and advertisers between them was fierce. And the *Examiner* was the home of yellow journalism, so stories like this were a dime a dozen. In the current climate where a Communist, a fellow-traveler, or a homosexual (and we were our own special category) might be suspected of reporting back to Soviet Russia or Red China, any story like this was damning in a way that was almost impossible to recover from. For me, it didn't matter. Rolling in money kept me insulated. But for most of the Joes and Janes out there, the possibility of this happening was a scary proposition.

As I stepped outside onto the windy street, I threw the rag into the first bin I saw, mad at myself for having spent an unnecessary nickel, and headed over to the first phone booth I could find.

I pulled the door closed and dropped in my dime. First things first. I called the office and Marnie picked up. "Nick Williams, Private Investigations," was the efficient greeting.

"It's Nick."

"Hi, Nick. New case with Klein?"

"Yeah. Say, remember Anna, that little girl with the polio?"

"Sure, I do. Sweet kid."

"Just ran into her pop, Tony, and he says she's doing better. Might be able to walk soon."

"Aww, that's great, Nick."

"Yeah. So, you think you could find something nice for a girl her age and have it sent over? I think you still have their address from before, right?"

"Oh, sure, Nick. Got it right here. He don't know it was you who paid all those bills, does he?"

"Doesn't look like it. You did a great job keeping that on the Q.T."

"That's swell. When I think of that—"

"Gotta go, Marnie. See you tomorrow. Go home when you're ready."

"Thanks Nick."

I hit the switch hook, waited for the tone, and dropped another dime. Now on to serious matters of another ilk. I rang up my buddy, Lieutenant Mike Robertson, to find out what the hell had happened with that raid. The desk sergeant answered and reported that Mike was out on a call. I left my name and number and asked for a call back. I heard the sergeant snicker as he hung up.

That made me think again about the front page picture and all those guys trying to hide their faces behind their hats as they were loaded into the paddy wagon, only to have their names, addresses, and places of employment all listed just below to make sure that Hearst rubbed it in and did it hard. No mercy. I kicked the side of the phone booth for good measure and then slammed open the door as hard as I could.

A passing stranger said, "You better be careful, mister, you could have a heart attack if you don't take it easy."

I took a deep breath and said, "Thanks, buddy. You're right about that." I turned towards Market Street so I could grab the streetcar and get home.

. . .

We lived at 137 Hartford Street in the unassuming and quiet neighborhood of Eureka Valley, just below where Market Street started its climb up the hill to become Portola, high above the city below. Our neighbors were a mish-mash of mostly Italian and Irish families whose children had mostly left home to move to more fashionable spots like Daly City and San Rafael.

The streetcar dropped me off at Castro Street. I walked across Market, down 17th Street to Hartford, and then up a block and a half to our modest bungalow on the left. It was the one with the Buick that was really too big for the driveway.

When I opened the door to the house, I hollered, "Honey, I'm home!"

I heard a grunt from the basement. I threw my hat on the chair in the front hall, ran through the kitchen, and then bounded down the steps. I found Carter sitting on a bench doing two of his favorite things: lifting up weights and sweating. I stood in the doorway and asked, "How are you?"

He looked up at me and then dropped the weight on the concrete floor. I looked for a crack, but this time it didn't happen. I kept thinking the floor would open up one of those days, but so far no luck.

Carter looked at me and smiled. "I can already tell my day has been a whole hell of a lot better than yours. What's got a bee up in your bonnet, Nick?"

I kicked my shoe at nothing in particular and looked down at the floor. "Fucking cops."

Carter made a dismissive noise. "Now, you know, buddy boy, I don't take talk like that around here. We're respectful of the law in this house."

"Yeah, well, when the law respects us, I'll respect the law."

"Wanna tell me about it?"

"There was a raid at the Kit Kat Club last night, complete with newspaper headlines and photos and ruined lives. You know, the usual."

"Well, if those boys and girls would stay home and behave, then these things wouldn't happen." He grinned his good ole southern boy grin. I figured he was trying to get a rise out of me because I knew he didn't believe any of the bullshit that just came out of his pretty mouth.

"If, for one minute, I thought—"

"Woah, Nellie. Hold on. You know what I think and how I feel. I suppose you have a new client out of all this mess."

"Yeah. I went to see Jeffery today and he hired me. No expense spared."

Carter whistled. "So, who's the big-wig that got rustled with the rest of the cattle?"

I shook my head. "Can't tell you. You know how it is."

"Hush-hush and all that?"

"Brother, you have no idea."

Carter raised an eyebrow at me. "Hollywood?"

I shrugged.

"Studio money?"

I shrugged again.

"Well, shit." And he used three syllables to pronounce that last word, like the good ole boy from South Georgia that he was.

"How's the leg?"

"Well, if no fog rolls in tonight, I expect it will be pretty good. I had no idea when it got crushed by a fire truck that it would become a weather prediction device." He smiled his slow, southern smile at me.

It had the effect he was hoping for. I pulled off my tie, disposed of my coat, and we spent the next 30 minutes in the basement making a hell of a lot of noise. This was, according to the man himself, his first most favorite thing.

. . .

Later that night, we were curled up on the sofa listening to classical music on the radio, courtesy of

KEAR, when the phone rang. I moved my legs off Carter's lap, walked into the hallway, between the kitchen and the living room, where the phone had its own little alcove, and picked up the receiver.

"Yes?"

"Hold please for Dr. Williams."

I put the receiver back in its cradle.

"Who was it?" asked Carter.

"Wrong number." I stood there for a minute knowing it would ring again and it did.

The smooth, female voice was back. "Is this Nicholas Williams?"

"Who's asking?" I knew who was asking.

"This is Marlene Johnson, Dr. Williams' private secretary," came the polite answer.

"Then, no, this is not Nicholas Williams. Nicholas Williams was last seen floating on a raft off the island of Borneo and we have no knowledge of his whereabouts."

As I put the receiver back on the machine, I looked over at Carter who was standing in the hall, leaning against the wall. He looked at me and smiled.

"Your dad?"

"His secretary."

"I see." The phone rang again. "You going to answer it?"

"No. Since you're here, why don't you?"

He raised the one hand not holding his cane. "Me? No thanks."

"Well, then, I guess we can listen to the tolling of the bell."

It kept ringing. And then it stopped. I looked up at Carter and said, "5, 4, 3, 2, 1..." The phone started ringing again.

I looked down at it and studied the black Bakelite

device so courteously provided to us by Pacific Telephone at a monthly rental rate of $1.35, federal excise taxes not included.

Carter said, "God dammit," and grabbed the receiver. "What?"

He listened and said, "He's right here."

The voice on the phone was agitated about something. I let it work itself out while Carter held the phone in his outstretched hand.

Finally, I gave in and took it from him. He hobbled closer and began to rub my neck with his free hand. The smell of tiger liniment, which he got at some place in Chinatown, was strong but not unpleasant. I was beginning to like the smell, as a matter of fact. And it was always very soothing when Carter's big, hairy paw did its healing magic on my sore muscles.

Someone was speaking at the end of the line and I didn't want to listen. I just wanted to crawl in bed next to my man and repeat some of what we'd just done in the basement earlier, but then I heard the word, "Janet."

I finally spoke. "What about Janet?"

"If you would listen to me, Nicholas, I'll tell you," came the irritated reply.

"Go ahead."

"She's in the hospital. She was in a car accident and they don't know if she'll make it. I want you to go down there tonight and make peace with her."

I pulled the receiver away from my ear and looked at it as though I had suddenly realized I was holding a banana against my head. I was having a hard time understanding what he was saying.

I looked up at Carter and my face must have told the story. He took the receiver from my hand and spoke into it.

"Dr. Williams?" He used his 4-star southern voice knowing it would be needed. "Can you repeat the details?"

He listened and nodded, not daring to interrupt. Carter had been brought up well, which is why he would never return to the State of Georgia.

He said, "Thank you, we'll be leaving right away." An angry retort was the reply. Carter put the receiver down in its cradle and whispered, "And fuck you too, old man."

I leaned against the wall and started to cry.

Chapter 4

137 Hartford Street
Monday, May 11, 1953
Half past 9 in the evening

Since it was Carter's right leg that took all the damage, I had to drive. That was OK, since I needed something to do to keep my mind from going crazy.

Janet was at St. Mary's Hospital, over by Golden Gate Park. It wasn't a far drive. We probably should have taken a cab, but I wanted to pull out the Buick, so we did.

It was a nice convertible '52 Super. Green body with a sharp chrome grill and a white cloth top. I probably needed to start thinking about a new one at some point, but I liked this car. It was a long car for our short driveway and it would never fit in the garage but it rode smooth, was roomy, and it took the steep San Francisco hills in stride.

We made the loop of blocks around to Castro. As we

crossed Market and drove up the steep hill where Castro becomes Divisadero, I looked at the houses and apartment buildings with their homey lights and wondered how many of them had televisions and how many were to tuned in to watch America's favorite redhead, laugh at her zany antics, and sympathize with her long-suffering Cuban husband. Thoughts like this and whether it was time for an oil change and lube job on the car kept me from screaming obscenities at a God I didn't even believe in.

We entered the building and found Janet's room. A nurse told us it was family only so, instead of telling her to jump off the roof, I calmly said I was Janet's brother and that this was a cousin from Georgia. The woman calmly looked at me and then at Carter and asked, "And you two are related?" I nodded. "To each other?"

Carter said, "That's right, ma'am. We're a close family."

She looked back at me and dryly said, "I don't know what kind of story you're peddling but that poor girl needs someone by her side because she won't be lasting long and you're the first *family* who's come to see her, so go right on in."

I took a deep breath as Carter opened the door. Janet was the only patient in a room with four beds. She was by the window. Her face was bruised but otherwise seemed fine. I wondered how bad the internal injuries were then I decided I didn't want to know when I heard her breathing.

I had heard men breathe like that when I was in the Navy. They didn't call it a death rattle for no reason.

I walked over to her and carefully put my hand on her shoulder, which seemed like a spot that wasn't broken or battered too badly.

"They should never have let you drive in the first place. I told Dad that when you were learning to drive on that poor old Hudson Eight."

Janet smiled a little and said, very quietly, "Fuck you, Nick."

"There's my girl."

She smiled a little again, although it looked painful. Her eyes were closed and were the least bruised part of her face, but she didn't open them.

"Is Carter here?"

Carter said, "You mean your real close cousin from the south?"

She took in a painful breath and asked, "She bought that?"

I said, "Enough to let us in the door so we could see you, sweet cheeks."

"Listen." I moved in closer. Carter hobbled over to my side of the bed and stood behind me.

"Tell Dad something for me."

"What's that, Janet?"

"Tell him to go fuck himself."

Carter laughed quietly and I tried not to start wailing right on top of my baby sister. I couldn't believe the old man wasn't here. But I was glad too. Because if the last words on Janet's lips were going to be those, I might be able to live through this.

Carter answered for me, "Oh, we will."

"Promise?"

I said, "Promise."

Janet's eyes fluttered. Her body began to shake. And then everything was very quiet. She was gone.

. . .

I went to find the nurse and told her the news. This was a different nurse. She came in, took one look at Carter, and said, "Family only."

"We are family. He's my—"

Carter said, "I'll be outside." He hobbled over past me and was gone.

"Are you the brother?"

I nodded. Having been relegated to a role without even a name actually felt better. I didn't want to be "Nick" or "Nicholas." I just wanted to be "the brother."

"Well, I need you to sign some forms. Do you know what we're supposed to do with the body?"

"The body." Ah, yes. The lifeless, inanimate corpse on the bed that had just a moment earlier told me to tell my father to go fuck himself. I decided that this was the perfect moment to do so.

"My father will have to make those decisions. Where's the nearest payphone?"

She told me and I walked out into the hallway. Carter looked up at me and I said, "OK, cousin, we need to call the father about the body. Come on."

I heard him mutter, "Oh, shit," under his breath.

"Cousin, you have no idea."

When we got to the phone, I dropped my dime and called his office number. Even though it was late in the evening, I knew he would be there. And that Marlene would be with him.

When the line was answered, it was Marlene's polite, efficient voice that spoke. I figured she was probably a very nice person and didn't get paid enough in either cash or fringe benefits to be in the center of the latest battle in the ongoing War of the Williamses, so I just said, "This is the son. Put the father on the phone."

She made a sound but said nothing. I heard a hand cover over the mouthpiece and some discussion mumbled its way up the wire.

His voice spoke clearly and crisply. "Is it over?"

I sighed and said, "Yes. It was fast."

"Good."

"I have two messages for you. One is from the hospital."

"Yes?"

"They would like to have instructions on the disposal of the body."

There was a brief silence. "I see. I'll take care of that. What's the other message?"

"The other message is—"

Before I could say it, I saw Carter's big, thick finger press down on the hook, effectively ending the call and saving me the trouble of having a stroke right in the middle of a hospital which, if you think about it, would have been very convenient.

I looked up at the man I loved more than ever and said, "Thanks."

"Don't mention it. Now, let's go home and go to bed."

I nodded and we walked and hobbled our way out.

. . .

I pulled the Buick into the small driveway and walked up the steps with Carter. Standing in the doorway was my favorite cop in the world, Mike Robertson.

He was standing under the light, which we had failed to extinguish before leaving, smoking the stub-end of a cigar and reading a dime-store novel. He stashed the novel in his back pocket and crushed the cigar with his policeman's shoe as we hobbled and walked up the stairs.

Carter spoke first. "Hey, Mike."

"Carter." Mike nodded and smiled. "Looks like you're healing up nicely."

By this time we were all on the porch together. It was always amusing to me to be around these two giants at the same time. Carter was about 6 inches taller than me at 6'4" and Mike was about an inch taller than Carter. Both of them had the same muscular build.

But whereas Carter had easy-going southern boy good looks with sandy-blond hair, Mike was more of the scary but handsome type. He had a pronounced forehead, jet black hair, and piercing blue eyes. When he was happy, he was reasonably attractive. When he was unhappy, you began to think of terrorized villagers running to get out of his way.

Carter asked, "How about some rye and water?"

I unlocked the door, walking between the two behemoths who liked to play that game where they pretend they can't see me because I'm so short. Since I'm usually the tallest guy in the room in a city full of Italian and Irish immigrants, I find this mildly amusing. And anything that made me think of something or someone other than my baby sister was OK by me.

I pushed open the door and Mike asked, "Do you always leave the door open like that, Carter?"

Carter replied, "No. I guess the wind must have blown it open."

"You two think you're real clowns, don't you?"

Mike walked in behind me and asked, "Did you hear a high-pitched voice coming from somewhere?"

Carter closed the door and pulled me into a hug. "No. It was my husband here. And he ain't that small, truth be told."

"Husband?"

I pulled Carter's arms in tighter. "We thought we'd

try it on for size. What do you think? We can both be husbands."

"We are what we say we are."

"Have you been reading more of that Krishnamurti stuff you get down at the bookstore on Sacramento?"

"Well, you know me. I gotta have something to read all the time. And the occult or higher thought is just as good as Zane Grey."

I nodded. "Uh huh. I see. I'll be sure to send a note about that to the *New York Times Book Review* and see what they make of it."

"Did I hear mention of rye and water? Seems like the hospitality in this house is on a rapid decline."

I pulled away from Carter, tossed my hat on the table, threw my coat over the banister, and went over to the bar. While I built him a drink I asked Carter, "The usual?"

"No, not tonight." I wondered at that but agreed with him. I wanted to get drunk in the worst way, but it would have to be a real bender. Just a sip of rye or gin wasn't going to be enough.

Mike had made himself comfortable in one of the armchairs, coat and hat still on. I pulled the hat off his big head and put it on the hallway table. Then I handed him his drink. "You not drinking either?" he asked as he ran his hand through his hair.

I shook my head. "No. It's been a hell of a night and I need to either stay sober or go full on out."

Mike took a sip of his rye while Carter eased himself on the sofa where I joined him and leaned against him, feeling the warmth of his body coming through his shirt. He put his bum leg up on the table. I leaned forward and slid a pillow underneath it for support.

Mike asked, "What happened?"

Carter said, "Janet just died."

Mike looked at me and then back at Carter. "Just died? When?"

I said, flatly, "Tonight. About twenty minutes ago."

Mike put down his drink and said, "I'm so sorry to hear that. Do you want me to go? I'm sure you have family things to handle."

Carter said, "We are handling family matters. This is our family." He grabbed my right hand with his left and squeezed.

Chapter 5

137 Hartford Street
Monday, May 11, 1953
Later that evening

We told Mike the story of what had transpired in the last hour. Carter did most of the telling. I mostly let him hold my hand and listened to him recount our little adventures along the way starting with the many phone calls all the way to the message I never got to deliver.

Mike was laughing when we got to that part and that let me finally let go a bit. I started laughing but found myself crying. I leaned in under Carter's muscular arm and let him hold me for a moment.

Mike stood up and I said, "Don't go." I sniffled and sat up straight. "I need to talk to you about why you're actually here."

Carter took hold of his cane and pulled himself up. "Since I know that this will be a private conversation,

I'm gonna hobble myself up to bed. Goodnight, Mike. Always great to see you." He patted Mike on his shoulder as he walked by. I watched him hobble up the stairs and then listened as he closed the bedroom door.

Mike said, "He's looking a lot better."

I nodded. "He's feeling a lot better. He's a real trooper and is spending a lot of time downstairs, working on his muscles."

Mike smiled. "That can't be all bad for you."

I smiled back and said, "It has its unforeseen benefits."

Mike raised his head up, like he did when he was about to talk about something unpleasant.

"I guess you called me about the raid last night."

I nodded. Grief, which had been interrupted by companionship and laughter, was now mutating into low-intensity anger. I had to remind myself, "*This is my friend. He was once my lover. He's one of us. Just listen and find out what he says.*"

He said, "You know I had nothing to do with that."

I nodded.

"It's the fucking *Examiner*. They are riding the brass from the mayor to the chief of police and all over town. Everyone's nervous."

I nodded.

"We didn't call the papers. Someone else did. We wanted to go in, do it quickly, issue bench warrants, and go on."

I nodded and took a deep breath.

Mike looked at me guiltily. "Who's your client?"

I was doing pretty good, so far. "Number 21."

"Oh shit. How do you even know about that?"

"Metro has deep pockets and they clean up their stars' messes real neat. Even way up here in the City by the Bay."

Mike nodded. He looked at his empty glass. "Can I help myself to another?"

"Sure. Go ahead." I was still OK, but it was getting harder to keep it all in.

Mike stood up and walked over to the bar. He poured about two fingers and then popped a splash of soda from the siphon.

I knew he was feeling bad. That was a lot of liquor for Mike Robertson. And he was probably still on duty. I wanted to say, "Take it easy. It isn't your fault. Damn those rags!" But I couldn't bring myself to do it.

I took another deep breath as Mike lowered his massive form into the armchair. This was one house he knew he could relax in since all the furniture was already giant-tested and approved by Carter.

I wanted to get in his face and scream at him. But I didn't. I just watched him squirm. I knew, in fact, that, by not getting angry, I was torturing him. He could deal with anger and righteous indignation. Silence, on the other hand, particularly mine, was not easy for him to handle.

"So, what does your client need?"

"We need to know who it is in the department that tipped off Metro."

A ball of confusion settled on Mike's face. "Well, why don't you ask... your client?"

"He's in Hollywood. Doing whatever it is that Hollywood types do."

Mike looked at his watch. "Well, I can tell you he's in bed and been in bed for hours. They roll up the sidewalks early in that town—"

"Goddam you, Mike!" It finally burst out.

He grimaced but looked oddly relaxed. Now we were in a place he knew he could handle.

"Calm down, Nick."

I simmered and stewed a bit.

"Those men. Their lives are ruined! Ruined!" I was really howling. I heard a cane hit the floor upstairs.

Mike put out his hand. "I know, Nick. I didn't do that. I don't know who did."

I nodded. "Were you at the scene? Were you the arresting officer?"

Mike said, "You know how it works. I was supervising. It was the beat cops who did the arresting."

"Then who tipped off the papers, Mike? Who?"

He shrugged and took a sip. "I dunno."

I took a breath and regrouped. "I know this isn't your fault. But someone, somewhere, sometime has to finally stand up and say that we will not be used to sell papers, to get out the vote, or thrown around as political fodder."

Mike said, "I agree. I'm doing my part. You know that."

I looked at him and could feel the cool returning. I knew he was a good cop. I knew he did good work. I knew he was not hiding himself from anyone. And he needed to be told that I knew. So I did.

Mike relaxed and, finally, after I'd laid it on a bit thick, said, "Hey Nick! I get the message. I'm a good cop. I know. Or at least I try to be."

I said, "And you are. I'm sorry I blew up at you."

"I don't blame you. I'm the only cop around, so you get to be mad at me. Believe me, Nick, I want to find out what happened just as much as you do. I know why. We all know why."

I said, "Right. Now let's find out who."

He took another sip. "Ben White."

"Who?"

"Ben White. That's Metro's mole."

I nodded. It made sense. He was the go-to guy for any time a studio or production company wanted to film in San Francisco and needed the help of the police department. Talk was that he was involved in the development of a TV show based in the City and similar to Dragnet.

"Do you know him?" I asked.

"I've seen him around. He's at Central. I'm at North. So we don't pal around. But I'm sure I could set up a meeting for you."

"How so?"

Mike nodded with a grin.

"Another one?"

Mike smiled. "As a three-dollar bill. And, from what I've heard, if you bring Carter and another fireman along to double-date, you'll have Ben White eating out of your hand."

I laughed and said, "Well, he's got good taste, I'll give him that."

Mike stood up. "I'll call you in the next couple of days when I can get that set up." I stood up and we walked to the door. I handed him his hat from the table. He put his hand on my shoulder. "I'm sorry about your sister. That's tough."

I nodded and said, "Thanks. Have a good night, Mike."

He stepped out onto the porch and pulled up his lapels. "Kinda nippy out here."

I looked out and could feel that the temperature had dropped several degrees since we'd been home. "You need a coat? I'm sure Carter could loan you one of his."

"No. This is fine. I'll walk down to Market and get a cab."

"Good night, Mike."

He waved back as he walked down the hill.

. . .

I stripped off my clothes and hung up everything. I was down to my BVDs and ready to get warmed up next to a hot fireman.

Carter was awake and reading. It was his favorite book. It was some sort of fantasy, by an English author, and involved a ring and a dragon and some dwarves. He'd tried to explain it me once, but it was too complex for my tastes. I liked the hard-boiled stories, the harder the better. They were straightforward. You knew where you stood with the characters. Nothing magical going on there.

I slipped in bed and under Carter's waiting arm. "You have it out with Mike?" he asked.

"You should know. I heard your cane tap."

"I was wondering if I should come down there. But it sounded like everything got worked out."

"It did. He gave me the dope I was looking for."

"Uh huh. Son, you ever gonna tell me anything about this whoever he is that I'm not supposed to know anythin' about?"

"Not yet. But I will tell you this, I need you to find one of your buddies who has a hard-on for cops because sometime in the next week or so, we're going on a double-date."

"We are, are we?"

"Yes, sir, we are."

"And where might that be?"

"You know. We're going to your favorite place."

Carter pulled me in close. "Tell me like you love me, honey chile."

"Top of the Mark!"

Carter let out a rebel yell and then turned over and kissed me deeply in the way that only a promise for the best view in the world and a porterhouse steak can deliver.

Chapter 6

137 Hartford Street
Tuesday, May 12, 1953
A little after 3 in the afternoon

I checked in with Jeffery by phone the next afternoon. I started off by telling him everything I'd found out from Mike about the raid. He said some choice words about the muckrakers at the *Examiner*, which I heartily endorsed.

"Old man Hearst has been dead and buried for almost two years, but I guess his ghost is running that filthy rag. This is just the thing he'd blow his wad over."

I looked at the phone in disbelief and then asked, "Did you just say, 'blow his wad'?"

"Yes. What of it?"

I thought for a moment. It suddenly made sense.

"So, how long have you and Taylor Wells been an item? And how did you manage not to get pulled in with the other fishes two nights ago?"

There was a meaningful silence on the other end of the line.

"Jeffery? You there?"

"Damn you, Nick."

I laughed. "We should be celebrating! You're in love with the most famous homosexual in Christendom."

"You can't tell a soul, Nick. Not a one."

"Hey. These lips, they stay tightly closed. But how did you get out without getting caught at the Kit Kat?"

"I wasn't there, that's how." I wondered at that. Jeffery continued, "Does Carter know who your client is?"

"He's probably figured it out but only because I adamantly couldn't tell him. You know how it works these days. Not saying something can be as damning as spilling the whole mess of beans."

Jeffery sighed down the line. I heard some rustling of papers on his end.

"Wait."

I did as I was told.

"Janet is dead?"

"Yeah. Last night. Is it in the paper?"

"It's on the bottom of the front page of the *Chronicle*. Just a couple of paragraphs. Police investigating possible tampering with brakes. Why didn't you say something, Nick?"

I was quiet. What was there to say?

"Gee, pal. That really hurts." I wasn't sure if he meant her death or my silence or maybe both. "She was a great gal and a real friend. I'm sorry for you, buddy."

I was brief. "Thanks. When we have time for a drink or two or twenty, I'll tell you about the whole damn thing. Now, what's that about brakes?"

"Says here they found that the brake line had been cut on her car."

"So, it wasn't an accident?"
"Looks to me like it was murder."

...

Later that same day, I had a very brief call from Marlene, my father's private secretary. She conveyed her condolences and then informed me of the time and the place of the memorial. It would be Saturday at 12 noon at Grace Cathedral on Nob Hill. It was a tony place, just perfect for a Williams bon voyage even though we weren't Episcopalians. In the religion department, the family was officially neutral, unless some affiliation was useful for a business deal.

I asked about the police investigation. She referred me to one Lt. Michael Robertson, who had taken charge of the case.

I clicked on the phone to get a new line. When I heard the familiar whirring sound, I dialed up the North District office and talked to the same desk sergeant as the day before. This time my call went right through.

"Robertson," was the brief greeting.

"Hey, Mike."

"Nick. You were on my list to call next."

"So, what's this about Janet's car?"

"No doubt about it. Brake line was cut. And by somebody who knew what he was doing. Do you have any idea who it could be?"

I sighed and put my left hand over my face. This just kept getting worse and worse.

"No. No one I can think of right now. But you know us Williamses, even the ones who like each other aren't exactly having tea every day."

"I know, Nick. And this must hurt like hell."

"Have you talked to the old man?"

"And how. Or he's been talking to me. And my captain. And the chief. Yeah. It's been all Dr. Williams, all day long."

I laughed grimly. "Welcome to my family, Mike. It's a pretty awful place to visit. I hope you don't have to hang around for very long. How did you get the case, by the way?"

"Simple. I asked for it this morning once we knew it was a homicide. Said I knew the family already and that it would be easier to get access. The Williams clan ain't exactly known for being friendly and welcoming. I'm pretty sure I just made my captain real happy since that meant he didn't have to deal with it."

"Where did the accident happen?"

"Well, near as we can tell, she was coming out the Broadway tunnel and couldn't stop. A couple of witnesses said she blew through the light at Larkin and then Polk and then crashed into the side of an apartment building right at Van Ness.

"I'll tell you this much. She had her hand on the horn the whole time and kept bobbing and weaving to avoid pedestrians. One man said he was sure she intentionally crashed into the building to make sure she didn't run people down who were crossing the street at Van Ness."

"That sounds like Janet. But puzzle me this. Isn't that a flat stretch right in there?"

"Exactly. That's got me puzzled too. I had my guy looking to see if there was something funny about the accelerator. Nothing obvious so far. But right about now the boys down at the shop are taking her car apart to see what else might have kept the engine gunning."

"She could have downshifted to slow down."

"Not on this model. She had a '53 Buick Skylark

convertible. Must have been a beauty too. Had automatic transmission."

"Well, that's where your boys oughta look. Bet there's something fishy with that transmission. By the way, don't those go for something like five grand?"

"Or more. This one was decked out. The guys at the shop were all over it. Baby blue with a white top. I thought your sister was out of the family loot. Where did she get five grand for a new car?"

"Was it new?"

"I checked with McAlister Buick, over on Van Ness, and they said she went in there last year on the very day the new '53s were announced and plunked down the cash, the full amount, and ordered it brand-spanking new from Detroit. Even had her name engraved on the steering wheel."

"Cash?" I couldn't imagine where Janet had gotten that kind of money. I would have given her that much. I would have given her ten times that much. Hell, I'd tried to give her money any time I could. But she was too proud, she always told me. Wanted to make her own way, she'd said. And I knew Janet would've stopped taking my calls if I'd pushed too hard, so I didn't.

Mike said, "If you can find out anything from the old man, I'd appreciate it. He seems to think that my job is to investigate without asking any actual questions."

I said, "That sounds like my father. I'll try. But I don't think I'll be able to do much."

"Let me know what you find out. Meanwhile, I have a call into Ben White. I'll let you know what he says."

"By the way, as an additional inducement, be sure to mention that dinner is my treat and that we'll be dining at the Top of the Mark."

Mike whistled. "I know that's above Ben's pay grade.

So I'm sure that might be just the ticket, even without the other inducement."

"Carter is down at the firehouse right now, working on that very thing."

"He's fast."

"When there's a porterhouse at the Top of the Mark with his name on it, you'd be amazed how quickly he can move."

Mike laughed and then the line went dead.

I put the receiver down and thought about calling Marlene back to set up an appointment with my father. I picked up the black beast and then put it back down. Not now. Maybe later. But not now.

Chapter 7

137 Hartford Street
Tuesday, May 12, 1953
Just past 6 in the evening

I was in the kitchen, pulling together a chicken pot pie for dinner. It was one of my specialties and it fit the bill for Carter's constant demand for stick-to-your-ribs dining. He could eat like a horse and never showed anything but more muscles in the balance. I also threw together a chilled tossed green salad for some color and flavor. Carter wasn't a fan of garlic and I could never get enough of it. So, when we had a salad with dinner, I would toss my bowl with my garlic zinger dressing and his with a homemade buttermilk that I'd finally gotten bland enough for him to like.

I had just made the dressings for that evening and put them in the icebox to chill when the damn phone rang. I had a feeling about this call and I didn't like it.

It could be Marnie calling to tell me she was going

home. I hadn't gone into the office. Didn't feel like it. Didn't have to.

Then again, it could have been more in the string of increasingly bad news about Janet.

I shrugged in resignation, wiped my hands off, and picked up the receiver in the hallway.

"Yeah."

"Please hold for—"

"Marlene, we're practically related. You don't have to be professional when you call me. I promise not to be an asshole just because you're calling me on behalf of a real stone-cold bastard."

She actually giggled. I was beginning to like Marlene.

"He wants to talk to you."

"My name is Nick."

"He wants to talk to you, Nick."

"You deserve some sort of medal. I'm not sure what it is, but when I find out, I'm going to nominate you for it. Put him on."

The line went silent for a moment and then the gruff voice said, "Don't you know this Lieutenant Robertson?" The question was loaded with derision, scorn, and revulsion. He knew I knew Mike. He'd met Mike once. It wasn't pretty.

"Yes, Father, I do. And how are you today?"

"Don't be flip with me. I haven't the time. Why don't you light a fire under the man and get him to wrap up this investigation of whatever it is?"

"Mike's the best cop I know. He's being thorough. He told me they're taking apart Janet's car to see if they can find out why it didn't slow down."

"That's what he told me. What's taking so long? That's what I want to know."

I looked at my watch. "That accident happened less than 20 hours ago. They are moving fast, as these things go."

There was a dissatisfied grunt down the wire. "And, furthermore, where did Janet get six thousand dollars to buy a new car and twenty thousand to buy a house?"

The house was new to me. "I don't know. I was going to ask you the same question."

"So, you're telling me you didn't give it to her from your ill-gotten gains?"

I bypassed the ridiculousness of that last remark and said, "Janet would never let me give her anything out of my trust."

"Well, maybe she was wiser than I ever gave her credit for. I wouldn't take a penny of the money from that old decrepit either."

"Oh, really? That's why you and that gang of thugs you call siblings took me all the way to the California State Supreme Court? Just so you could say, 'No, I actually don't want any of it.'"

By the time I got the last sentence out, the line was dead. Pretty soon I heard the mechanical voice saying, "If you want to make a call, please hang up."

So I did just that.

. . .

About 10 minutes later, I was cooking up the vegetables I'd just chopped in some butter, getting them a little soft before stuffing them in the pie, when I heard the front door open and close and a sweet southern voice called out, "What smells so good?"

I said, "It's your favorite."

I heard the familiar tap of the cane but I also heard someone else walking across the living room floor.

I kept stirring, wondering who Carter had picked up down at the firehouse who might need a home-cooked meal.

Carter said, "Look who I ran into."

I turned around and smiled in genuine delight. "Well, look who the cat dragged in."

Henry Winters was Carter's ex. They had a history that went all the way back to primary school in Albany, Georgia. They were best friends through school and then lovers for a stint.

Henry and Carter had bought a used Ford, somehow driven it from South Georgia across the country, including the desert, and up the California coast to San Francisco in the summer of 1939.

Carter had signed up for fireman training as soon as he got to the City. When the war started, he'd tried to enlist, but the board wouldn't let him. Firemen, particularly along the West Coast, were needed where they were. If there was an enemy bombing, they were told, they would be much more valuable at home than anywhere they might go in Europe or the Pacific.

Henry had, at first, taken any odd job he could get. They had lived in a one-room affair in the Tenderloin, not far from my illustrious office, and had spent the nights alone together and the days working hard.

Eventually, Henry got his college degree in engineering at Cal and went into the Army in '43 as a captain. The war changed things between the two of them and so they parted after Henry got back in the fall of '45.

But they were still best friends and I was glad for that. I also never failed to notice how very much alike we two looked. Both of us stood about 5'10" and lanky, with thick, dark hair. I'm pretty sure we could have swapped out clothes easily. The only real difference was in the color of our eyes. Mine are brown and his are green. And he has a souvenir from the war where he got into a fight with a German officer he was trying to arrest. He has a long scar along the right side of his face. It actually enhances his good looks.

I once was teasing Carter and asked him if he'd broken it off with Henry because of the scar. The response I got assured me that was not the case, thank you very much, and it really angered him on and off for several days. I didn't know him well enough at the time to be able to figure out whether I'd hit the mark or whether I'd deeply offended Carter's sense of propriety. Now I knew it was the latter.

Henry had taken on a master's degree after the war and was now working at a little place called Bechtel.

"I hope I'm not intruding, Nick."

I turned down the gas, wiped my hands, and walked around the table to greet him. I gave him a hug and said, "You know you're always welcome here anytime, Henry."

He looked a little doubtful.

I said, "Seriously. I love you just like Carter does. We're family."

Henry looked at me and said, "I'm so sorry about Janet."

I nodded and didn't say anything. I turned towards the hallway and asked, "Who wants a drink?"

I heard Henry call out, "Gin and tonic, if you have it."

I said, "Sure thing. How about you, Carter?"

"I'm good for a beer."

I heard him open the icebox and grab a bottle.

As I was building Henry's drink, I called out, "What's the latest in your world, Henry?"

Carter called back, "That's why he's here, Nick."

I grabbed the tumbler and walked back into the kitchen. Henry was sitting at the table, looking miserable.

I handed him the drink and asked, "What's got you

down, Henry?"

Carter sat down at the table and slammed his beer. "Fucking F.B.I."

I said, "I thought we didn't talk about cops like that in this house?"

Carter said, "Well, I'm beginning to think otherwise."

I went back to the stove to finish putting the pie together. The oven was beginning to heat up the room, so I walked over to the sink and raised up the window a bit. I could hear the girls next door calling out to one of their poodles, "Mitzi!"

Henry said, in a low voice, "I've been let go from Bechtel."

I turned around and asked, "What? Why?"

"Because I'm a homo. And that's a direct quote."

Carter looked grim. My first thought was that this might affect his own job, whenever he was ready to go back.

Carter looked at me and said, "The feds are cracking down on us subversive types. Henry's been working on a sensitive project and they just did a deep review of all the senior staff, looking for"—I looked at Carter sternly, who knew why—"um, what they could find in the woodpile."

Henry said, in a mocking tone, "This ain't Georgia, boy."

Carter nodded. "I know. Just a force of habit, I guess." He sighed.

I brought the conversation back to the topic. "Look. They can't just fire you like that, can they? You're one of the best. Old man Bechtel even said so."

Henry shrugged. "Yes, they can. When there's millions of dollars of contracts at stake, you bet they can." He sighed deeply. "I'm never going to work as an engineer again."

I said, "Well, pardon my French, but fuck that shit. How hard is it to start your own firm?"

I was back at the stove, tucking in all the goodies. I went over to the icebox and got more butter and the bottle of milk. Time to make the white sauce for it all to simmer in.

"Jesus, Nick. I don't know."

I reached for the canister of flour. "Well, you have the contacts for at least one job, right?"

"Probably more than one. But I don't have the money to do that."

I turned on the gas and cut in some of the butter and poured in a little milk. I began whisking the two together.

"Well, I do. And it's just sitting there, getting bigger and bigger every day. Why not start your own firm? I'll underwrite you till you get on your own feet and you can pay me back whenever. Or you can bring me in as a silent partner. Whatever you prefer."

I took a tablespoon of flour to start the roux.

"Are you serious, Nick?" asked Henry.

"I sure am. Just don't ask me to do any work."

"Well, that's swell, Nick. That's swell!" I was standing over the stove so I couldn't see his face, but it sounded like he was happy, which was nice. Someone in that room deserved to be happy.

"You decide how you want to set things up and then call Jeffery. He'll take care of all the paperwork and I'll cover his initial fees as an early Christmas present. Then, when you're ready, we'll sign the papers, I'll cut you a check, and you can start picking out furniture for your new office."

By this time the roux was beginning to stretch out. As Henry and Carter started talking about where to put in an office and who to approach for projects, I added a bit more flour and then some butter and another drop of milk. Once it was time, I added more milk and pulled that all together with the whisk. I poured the satiny mixture over the chopped chicken and vegetables, then covered that with the top layer of pastry, put the whole mess in the oven, and had a seat at the table.

Those two Georgia boys looked very happy. And that made me smile.

Chapter 8

137 Hartford Street
Wednesday, May 13, 1953
Half past 9 in the morning

The next day was Wednesday and I was in no mood to be in the office. I called Marnie early while she was still at home and told her to take the day off with pay. We were closed until further notice. Besides, the service could pick up any calls.

After I got off the phone with her, the instrument started ringing again. I grimaced, not liking the sound of the bell, and picked up the receiver.

"Yeah?"
"Nick? It's Jeffery."
"Good morning, sunshine."
"And to you."
"Oh, you have company?"
"Why yes. If you wouldn't mind joining us at 10 am, I'm sure that would be perfect."

"And who is us?"

"Why, Mr. Mannix, of course."

I said a few choice words down the line. I couldn't believe it. This was exactly what I didn't want when he got me mixed up in this screwball case.

"You'll be here by then?"

"Of course. And then I'm going to kick your ass all the way to Sausalito."

"Wonderful. Looking forward to seeing you too. Goodbye."

The line went dead before I could share any further choice words.

Eddie Mannix was Metro's fixer. Whenever one of their stable went on a bender or slept with a person possessing the wrong genitalia or stole something from a downtown department store, Eddie went behind them and made sure to clean up whatever mess he or she left behind.

This was great for the stars and starlets but pretty bad for the ones who happened to be standing in the spot where the fix got applied. Plus, Mannix was a Grade A, Number 1 hater of all things queer, fag, or fairy. And he didn't mind telling me to my face.

Which he had done before. When something very similar had happened here in our fair city not too long ago, Jeffery had handled the courts and I had worked with Mike to sort things out with the police. And then descended Mannix, like an avenging angel, to scream at both of us, since all we'd done was his job, and then he'd thrown a huge check in both our faces.

I decided that sharp blue was the color of the day and got myself dressed and out the door by 9:30. I pulled out the Buick and drove up Hartford, made a right on 18th Street, another right on Castro, then down a block to Market.

As I drove down Castro, very slowly behind a truck that couldn't seem to shift up out of first gear, I watched the neighborhood ladies doing their morning shopping. First it was the supermarket then it was either the fish and poultry man or the butcher. Maybe a stop at the bakery for some delectables to be served at afternoon mahjong or the local women's auxiliary of whatever fraternal organization their husbands had pledged. I knew most of these ladies by sight, although we'd never really been introduced. They had their world with their teas, mass, Friday suppers, and such. And I had my world with my husband and his dick in my mouth. The two were not likely to mix.

Besides, I didn't really want all the ladies up and down Hartford, over on Collingwood, and throughout the neighborhood to know that one of the wealthiest men in America, and definitely the wealthiest queer possibly since Alexander the Great, lived among them.

I'm sure they would have been perfectly nice, but I didn't want to have to answer a lot of questions or be hit up for solicitations.

The Williams Beneficial Foundation handled all that for me. It was right up there with the Carnegie Endowment in terms of giving. I got an invitation each year to their annual meeting, which I always politely declined, and received the annual report that followed said meeting, which I usually tossed in the bin.

It seems that Uncle Paul had literally taken all the gold rush money he'd inherited from his father and multiplied it many times over through shrewd investments, some unscrupulous money lending, and a lot of just being in the right place at the right time. He survived all the crashes that had preceded the big one and, from what I was told, had made money on the Depression, as had a few others.

I was thinking about all this when the light turned green at Market and I failed to notice. Fortunately, a kind soul reminded me by laying on their horn.

Ten minutes later, I was crawling up Market Street. I'd managed to cross Van Ness without incident, but then the combination of delivery trucks, slow-moving and overburdened streetcars, and the general mass of automobiles brought everything to a stop.

I checked my watch and realized I was going to be late. Oh ducky.

. . .

I rolled into Jeffery's conference room at 10:15. Robert had a frown on his otherwise pretty face when I walked through the door.

I asked, "That bad?"

"Much worse, Mr. Williams. Much worse."

I could hear the noise all the way out in front. I soldiered on and burst in without bothering to knock.

At the table were, from left to right: Eddie Mannix, asshole extraordinaire, Taylor Wells, glamour guy of the moment, and Jeffery Klein, much put-upon attorney and erstwhile lover of said Taylor Wells.

Eddie was purple and was screaming, "Why can't you two fairies keep it in your pants?"

I said, cheerily, "Morning all!"

Taylor smiled at me weakly. Jeffery looked like he was ready to be boiled in oil, which would have been preferable to what he was experiencing. Mannix turned on me.

"Now we have all the fruits in one room. Great! We have the whole fruit salad."

"Hi Eddie. Good to see you again too."

I sat down across from Taylor and between Jeffery and Mannix.

"What I want to know is when were you gonna tell me about your newest lover boy?" This question was directed at Taylor, who just shrugged.

Jeffery started to speak, but Mannix got there first. "I don't wanna hear nuthin' from you. This is a pure conflict of interest. I should fire you right here and now."

I spoke up. "But you won't, Eddie, right? Because it takes a cocksucker to help a cocksucker and that's the problem you have here."

Eddie turned on me and burned. He looked at me hard and quietly said, "We don't need that kind of fixin' in this case. This son of a bitch"—he was pointing at Jeffery—"he could queer everything for us." Mannix laughed, alone, at his inadvertent joke. He pulled out a pack of Pall Mall and quickly lit a cigarette. He then pointed it at Jeffery. "Someday your cover is gonna be blown and I'm gonna be very happy to watch you come tumblin' down, you fuckin' fag."

I stood up, pushed in my chair, and leaned against the wall. I crossed my arms and looked at Mannix. "Then why are you here, Eddie? Why don't you just fire Jeffery, and me, and do us all a big favor?"

Eddie looked up at me with hatred in his eyes. "Because you're all I've got right now." He spoke slow and steady. I knew he had a heart condition and was hoping he'd brought his pills because he was about to need them.

I nodded, still smiling, and started in on the only thing that would shut Mannix up: a steamroll. "So you do need Jeffery and me, doncha? Like I said before, you need one to handle one. We may be queer but Jeffery knows his way around the odd thing known as the justice system in this town. And you benefit from it." I looked him dead in the eyes.

"And, I often wonder, Eddie, what it is that you go back to Hollywood and say to Mr. Schary about your meetings up here in Baghdad by the Bay that justifies your outrageous salary."

Mannix was strangely quiet for a moment. I grabbed one of the red apples that was in the middle of the table and began to polish it on my coat sleeve.

I pressed on. "I hope that, at least while you're up here, you'll take a stroll through Golden Gate Park and visit the Oriental Tea Garden. Oops! I mean the recently re-named and restored Japanese Tea Garden. Beautiful spot. So glad they didn't pull the whole thing down during the war. Would have been a shame."

I bit hard into the apple and looked at Mannix, who now seriously looked like he was having a heart attack.

"And how is your wife?"

With that, Eddie lunged up out of his chair. But he was an older man who was not accustomed to long marathons of sex with another man, so his body didn't go as far as his mind wanted it to. I sidestepped. He tripped and fell on his knees, breathing hard. Taylor rushed around the table and helped Mannix up.

"I oughta clean your clock, you pansy. How dare you bring my wife into this?"

I just shrugged. "And, when you get back to Hollywood, which I assume you are about to do, and on the very next plane, will you give my regards to George Reeves? I've had such a crush on him ever since I saw him in those tight riding breeches in *Gone with the Wind*." I winked at Eddie and walked out of the conference room.

I sat in my usual spot in Jeffery's office, looked out the window at the beautiful blue waters of the bay, and waited for the mess in the other room to be over.

I didn't have to wait long. In about 10 minutes,

Taylor and Jeffery came into the office.

I grinned as they both walked around and stood in front of me. Jeffery tried to thunder down on me, but I was having none of it.

"Damn it, Nick! Why'd you have to do a thing like that?"

"Because that officious prick has the nerve to pick on the two of you while he's got his Japanese mistress stashed up at the Palace and his wife and George Reeves are probably canoodling right now up in Tahoe."

I took another bite out of my apple.

Taylor looked scared. Jeffery was a cross between angry and relieved.

I stood up and threw the apple in the bin. I reached over and pulled Taylor into an embrace, dipped him, and kissed him right on the mouth, without any tongue, of course, that wouldn't have been gentlemanly.

I noticed he didn't refuse and he knew how to dip backwards. I pulled him back up and then pushed him towards Jeffery.

"You're welcome, kid. Now be good to my friend or I will hunt you down and kick your ass."

I straightened out my coat and pulled down my sleeves. I looked over at Jeffery who was trying very hard not to laugh.

Chapter 9

137 Hartford Street
Friday, May 15, 1953
About half past 7 in the morning

Friday morning dawned cloudy and dull. We'd been having so many sunny days in a row, I'd almost forgotten that it might not be bright in the bedroom when I woke up.

Carter was snoring, lightly, when I opened my eyes. I got out of bed, ever so quietly, and ran the water in the shower.

As I was brushing my teeth, waiting for the hot water, Carter came in and began to relieve himself. He stood there sleepily, bracing himself against the wall for support. I rinsed off my brush, dropped it in the glass, and walked into the shower.

A couple of years ago, we'd discovered that neither of us liked baths. We finally figured out we could take out the old, cast iron bathtub and tile the wall and floor and install a walk-in shower. Best five hundred bucks I ever spent.

Carter followed me into the shower, reached above my head, and redirected the nozzle up.

"You know I hate it when you do that."

"I know." He yawned and then moved the nozzle even higher so it would spray him in the face. I reached up and he swatted my hand out of the way.

"Look you," I threatened.

"Yeah? What're you gonna do about it?"

I had a few suggestions and Carter decided to take matters into his own hands. That was one of the many reasons why I loved him.

Twenty minutes later, we'd long ago drained the water heater but were cleaning up from being frisky in the morning. It was a brisk change to have a nice cold shower on a foggy morning. And I wouldn't have had it any other way.

We were both getting dressed when the goddam phone rang.

I said, "Let it ring. If they need to talk to us, they'll call back."

"We really need an upstairs extension."

"Why don't you call Pacific Telephone and have them bring out some sweet phone repairman to install one? Sounds like a project just up your alley."

Carter asked, "What if they bring out a sweet phone repair lady?"

"Send her next door."

I was referring to our only real neighborly neighbors, a "lady couple," as Carter liked to refer to them. They were Pam and Diane. Pam was an actual honest-to-god construction worker. She was nimble as a goat, not afraid of heights, a member of the union in good standing, and knew how to throw a mean left hook if hassled. Diane taught the fourth grade at the neighborhood primary school over on Collingwood.

They had two poodles that I was mostly disinterested in but that Carter thought were cute. They adored him and treated me with the same indifference I had for them.

Pam was from Idaho, from some crazy family whose drama was right up there with mine. Diane moved to the Bay Area from Modesto and came from an Okie family. She was born in Enid and had been thirteen in '35 when the family finally took to the road and found their way out of the dust bowl and into the Central Valley.

They were wonderful neighbors. Friendly when engaged, nosy about everyone but us, and willing to serve as dates on the very rare occasions when we just couldn't do anything different. Usually those involved something swank with the firemen's union. I would foot the bill for whatever new outfits were needed, including paying Diane for nuisance time when she had to drag Pam to a dress shop once. We had gone to an event at the Legion of Honor and a new dress was de rigueur.

The phone had stopped ringing but then it rang again. I was only in my shirt and BVDs, but I went down the stairs, two at a time, cursing whoever was calling.

I picked up the black devil and said, "Yeah?"

"And a good morning to you too."

"Sorry, Mike. How are you?"

"I'm good and I have good news for you on two fronts."

"Shoot."

"First, we found out what happened to the transmission on Janet's car."

"Really, what was it?"

"It had been rigged to stay in motion."

"How does that work?"

"Beats me. But that's what the boys at the shop say."

"Sounds like something only a professional could do."

"Right."

"Have you tried to trace the money that Janet used to buy the car?"

"I'm still working on it. I just got the subpoena today for Hibernia Bank to open up her account records."

"Hibernia?"accoun

"Why? What's strange about that?"

"Nothing except she has an account at Bank of America. Every Williams has banked there since it was Bank of Italy."

"Maybe that was part of her rebellion."

"Maybe... Did you know she also bought a house? With cash?"

"Yes. Does that surprise you?"

"Damn right it does. This is a girl who was known to be ecstatic when she had fifty bucks to her name. I don't get it."

"Well, I'll be finding out about it in an hour or so. In fact, her branch was on Castro and 18th Street. You still playing hooky?"

"No. I gotta go in and answer mail and make sure Marnie doesn't knit herself a noose and hang herself."

Mike laughed.

"What's the other piece of good news?"

"Oh, are you and Carter free for dinner tonight?"

"Sure. Where do you want to go?"

"Oh, not me, buddy boy. I'm talking about Ben White."

"Oh, right. He's available tonight?"

"Yes. And you better make sure to deliver on the

location and the, you know, other thing."

"I think Carter has that covered and we're definitely on for 7 pm at the Top of the Mark. When are they gonna give you your own office?"

"Hell if I know. Say, how did you know tonight would be the night?"

"I didn't."

"Then how do you already have reservations at the hottest spot in town at 7 pm on a Friday night?"

"I don't. Didn't you hear? My name is Nicholas Williams, and I'm the richest fag in town. Don't worry. I know the maitre d' there. We'll be waiting for Ben at the bar. Tell him to dress sharp."

"Will do."

"Call me at the office if you find anything interesting at the bank, will you?"

"You'll be the first to know."

With that, he dropped the receiver and the line went dead.

Carter was coming down the stairs, heavy on the cane.

"Do you have a sucker lined up for tonight? We're go with Ben White for dinner."

Carter came around the corner and grinned at me. "I sure do and you won't guess who."

I liked it when Carter put on a suit, which wasn't often these days since dungarees were the best clothes to wear to a soggy, muddy, soot-covered crime scene. Usually, he had an old wool pullover on top of a couple of T-shirts for layers, depending on the weather. He had a pair of monster boots that were probably designed for guys scaling telephone poles but he liked them because they didn't slip and that was important with his cane.

Today, however, he was wearing one of his tailored

suits. The cut and style were about two years out of season, but it looked good on him. My reaction was, as always, to look like the cat in the cartoon whose eyes bug out.

He reached over and ran his big hand up my shirt and rubbed my belly.

"So, who is it?"

"Well, the two usual suspects weren't available. Seems like one of 'em has decided he's back on girls."

"Oh, brother."

"It's a phase."

We both laughed.

"And the other one is shacking up with some artist type over on Potrero Hill."

"Well, how about that... I assume it's all goatees and painter's smocks and crepe-soled shoes?"

"More like construction gear. The artist builds massive sculptures out of copper. Lots of welding. Real butch, apparently."

"So, who does that leave us with?"

"Martinelli."

My eyes bugged out again.

"No!"

"Yes!"

"How did you even? I mean... What was that conversation?"

"Make me a cup of coffee and a couple of eggs and I'll tell you."

I looked down at my shirt and BVDs.

"Who's gonna see you?"

I looked around and said, "Right. Fuck 'em."

I walked into the kitchen and pulled out eggs, a rasher of bacon, butter, and the bottle of milk from the icebox.

I filled the percolator with water, put some coffee in

the top reservoir, and then plugged it in. I reached down under the cabinet and got out a bowl and started cracking eggs. "So, tell me about it. I thought Martinelli was a Kinsey zero. All he-man and stuff."

Carter laughed. "So did I. I was over at the firehouse yesterday and the other guys were sacked out. Martinelli and I were in the kitchen playing penny poker—"

"Civil servants gambling on the job?"

"Well, one was on the job. The other was loitering with intent."

"True. Go on."

I had started up the gas under the skillet and was waiting for it to get hot before I dropped in the bacon.

"Well, we're talking about this and that and suddenly I got an inspiration. I asked him, 'Did you ever think about what happens in a place like prison?'"

"You asked what?"

"I know. The words were out of my mouth before I'd realized what I'd said."

I laid out four strips of bacon and they began to sizzle. I opened the bread box and took out the cottage loaf I'd picked up the day before and began to cut some slices for toast under the broiler.

"So, obviously he didn't slug you since you don't have a black eye."

"No. It was anything but that."

"What?" I was almost breathless at this point. I turned the bacon. We may have had problems when it came to garlic but we both agreed: crispy bacon is the devil. It's chewy or nothing.

"Well, he stands up and comes over to give me a shoulder rub." When Carter said that, I turned around to look at him. He was wearing the South Georgia shit-kicking grin that I loved so much.

"What did you do, Mr. Jones?" I tried to use my schoolmarm voice, but it didn't work.

"Well, Mr. Williams, I said, 'Hey. I was asking for a friend.'"

"What did he say?" I picked up the bacon and put it on a towel to drain. I poured the grease into the can on the counter and then cut off some butter, put the skillet on the stove, and turned down the heat.

"He said, 'Yeah, I thought you were an item with that private dick.'"

"Let me guess, he emphasized the word 'dick'."

"You got it."

"Well, so he's up for meeting a rising star in the police department for a date tonight?"

"All I had to do was to mention the Top of the Mark."

I put in the toast under the broiler and then turned the beaten eggs into the skillet. In about five more minutes, we were tucked in to our breakfast.

Chapter 10

137 Hartford Street
Friday, May 15, 1953
About half past 8 or so

Carter, who liked red plum jam above all other jams and jellies, was about to lick his middle finger, which was covered in the red goo, when I intercepted his hand and did it for him.

We were sitting like this when I heard a knock on the front door.

I sighed and said, "You have to answer it."

He grunted, pulled on his dick to get it back into place as he stood up, and hobbled to the front door.

I heard a high feminine voice say, "Hi, Carter. Hope I'm not bothering you boys this morning. I threw Mitzi's ball too high and it's in your backyard."

Carter said, "Good morning, Diane. Aren't you going to be late to school?"

She giggled. "Probably, but Mitzi will tear up our

living room furniture if she doesn't have her ball."

The voices got closer as they walked towards the kitchen. Diane came in and said, "Hi, Nick. Sorry to bother you boys."

She was a cute thing. She was petite and stood at about Carter's elbow. She was wearing a pink and red dress she'd made herself that was cute in 1950 and was still fine today, only she needed to bring up the hem a couple of inches. She was wearing sensible oxfords, being smart enough to know that standing on your feet all day could be hell on your feet. Her hair was a mass of blonde curls that she tried to manage in a number of ways. That morning she had most of it pinned back up off her face. I always thought that was the most attractive look for her.

I said, "It's no bother as long as you don't mind if I don't get up. I'm not dressed yet."

She giggled again. "Oh, that's fine."

Carter said, "Hold on just one minute, Diane. I'll go get Dame Mitzi's ball for you."

With that, he went out the back door and hobbled down the steps to go find it.

"Have a seat. And help yourself to coffee if you want some. Again, it's better if I don't get up."

She giggled and said, "No coffee for me this morning. I've already had two cups and Pam says I really need to cut back."

Then she frowned. "Oh, gee, Nick. I'm so sorry. I read all about your sister. That's tough. I'm real sorry. So is Pam. She told me to tell you so. I asked her if I should bring you a casserole or something and she said that would be like bringing a tuna fish sandwich to The Palace. And I guess she's right. You're such a good cook and all that."

I loved Diane. She usually went as my date. But Pam

was right. The girl needed to cut back on her coffee intake.

"Thanks, Diane. I appreciate the sentiment."

"I read that the memorial is tomorrow afternoon at Grace Cathedral. I'll bet there'll be some crowd there. Your family. Gee, I still can't believe you live here and not in some fancy mansion on Nob Hill. I was just telling Pam the other day how nice it was that you and Carter lived next door to us. Makes the neighborhood more neighborly like that, don't you think?"

I smiled and wondered where Carter was. "I do. You two are the best neighbors we could have."

She giggled for the fifth time. "Well, we love you guys. And I still think it was so funny the way you gave me that check, which we really needed at the time by the way, and put 'Pain and Suffering' in the memo. Pam's difficult but I have my ways. Just don't tell her anything about that."

I shook my head solemnly. "Mum's the word."

Carter walked in right then and I was vastly relieved. He handed over the red ball, which, of course, was covered with slobber and morning dew and bits of grass from when Manuel had cut the yard the day before. Just the thing for him to handle and perfectly fine for me to never, ever touch.

"Well, I'd better go. I'm sure that mean old principal is gonna be mad that I'm late again." She giggled.

"What about your students?" asked Carter as he expertly guided her into the hallway and on her way out the door.

"Oh, they love it when I'm late. They always pretend like I'm in the ladies and they're quiet as mice. But I think the principal knows anyway. OK, thanks, Carter." She yelled in my direction. "Bye, Nick. Thanks again!"

I waved in that direction, knowing she wouldn't see

me and would have forgotten about me anyway as she ran next door, up the stairs, and delivered the royal gem to her majesty, Queen Mitzi.

Carter hobbled back in and grinned.

I stood up and started clearing plates.

He said, "You go upstairs and get dressed. I'll take care of this."

"Are you sure?"

"Sure. Doctor Mullins told me yesterday to move around in different ways. He said it could help strengthen my leg."

I said, "OK." I reached up on my toes and gave him a kiss. "You should get an award for best neighbor ever."

He swatted me on the behind as I turned to go upstairs.

. . .

I rolled into my office around 10 am. Marnie was there and was on the phone. She said, "He just walked in the door, Mike."

I walked into my office, put my hat on the rack, took a seat, and picked up the receiver.

"What'd you find, Mike?"

"You won't believe this. Are you sitting down?"

"Sure." But I sat up straight.

"Your sister got a series of wire transfers in from some bank in Switzerland last year. All in all, the deposits were close to five hundred grand."

"Are you serious?"

I could hear the street noise. I figured he was standing in the booth right next to the Hibernia branch on Castro.

"You bet. What's more, it came from a numbered account."

"What does that mean?"

"Whoever had the account is anonymous and no amount of pleading or crying can make the bank or the Swiss government tell who owned the account because they don't know."

"That's like those Nazi accounts."

"Right. You don't think?"

"Of course not. This smells like Uncle Paul, to tell you the truth. Janet turned 25 last year."

"When was her birthday?"

"April 19th. Why?"

"Well, because the first of the deposits hit her account on April 21st."

I looked at the previous year's calendar. "That makes sense. April 21st was a Monday. Her birthday was on a Saturday."

"Do you remember her saying anything about getting some money for her birthday?"

I thought for a moment. "I don't think I saw her for her birthday last year."

"Your own sister?"

"That's the Williamses for you. Like I said, even though she and I were probably as close as any two siblings in our wretched family have been for generations, we still hardly saw each other. Too many bad memories."

"Gee, Nick. I knew it was bad but I didn't know it was that bad."

"Well, when your own father sues you in probate court... You get the picture."

"Sure. Well, I wanted to tell you about this as soon as I could. If you find out anything from your end, let me know, will you? Your dad is breathing down my neck again."

"I'll call him right now. I want to tell him about the money before anyone else does. I want to hear how he reacts. You wouldn't know what to listen for."

"Thanks, Nick. Saves me the trouble, and I mean trouble, of having to call him."

"No problem."

"Say, so who's the guy that Carter found for Ben White?"

I laughed. "He's the one guy neither of us would have ever expected. Tried to give Carter a rubdown yesterday but was persuaded to put on his best duds and meet us at the Mark Hopkins instead. Speaking of which, I need to call them. Gotta go, Mike. Thanks for the call."

"Any time, Nick."

And, with that, I dropped the receiver.

"Marnie!"

"Yeah, Nick?" came the answer as she walked in.

"Any mail I need to see?"

"Nothing really. I paid all the bills. The rest was trash."

"Good girl. Get me the maitre d' at the Top of the Mark on the phone, will ya?"

Her eyes lit up. "You and Carter going on a date tonight?"

"A double-date. We're hooking up a cop with a fireman."

"Ooh! That sounds dreamy."

"Oh, Marnie. We need to find you a guy."

"No thanks, Nick. I've got my mother and that's plenty for me."

"Sometime you gotta tell me who broke your heart."

She clammed up, which was always startling to witness. "Some other time, Nick. Let me get you that hoity-toity on the phone."

I sat back in the chair and put my feet up on the desk. I tried to figure out who would have set up a bequest like that for Janet and whether that's why she was killed. If she died, who benefited under the terms? Suddenly I realized I needed to get over to her house. Right away.

The phone rang. I had to take this one, however. I picked up and Marnie said, "Please hold for Nick Williams."

I heard a click and then Marcel spoke. "Ah, Mr. Williams, what a pleasure to hear from you."

"Thanks, Marcel. Look, I need the very best table for four that you have tonight at 7 pm. I've got a hundred bucks for you if you can swing it."

"For you, Mr. Williams, I certainly can. I see... *Alors*... Mr. Hearst is bringing his younger brother... And they have... Hold one moment." The line went silent and I thought to myself that if there was any justice in this world then I was about to bump that bastard Hearst from his table.

Marcel came back on the line. "I see that Mr. Hearst and party had an unexpected cancellation." That meant that Marcel had moved them around. They would be there and they would be glaring at us but we would be there at the best table, all four of us big queers having a wonderful time and hopefully sparking a romance, and there wouldn't be a damn thing any of them could do about it. Besides, I knew enough about the guy to know he was a lousy tipper.

Chapter 11

777 Bush Street
Friday, May 15, 1953
Just past 1 in the afternoon

I jumped up after I put the phone down and grabbed my hat. I realized I didn't have my gun and, more importantly, I had no idea where Janet lived.

As I was walking out I gave Marnie some instructions.

"Call St. Mary's and tell them you're following up on some of the details about Janet Williams. Tell them you're calling from Dr. Williams's office."

"Uh huh."

"I need to find out what address they have on file with her. If they don't have it or won't give it, call the county tax assessor and ask them. Promise anything to anyone. No amount of money is too high. I need that address. And I need it now."

"But where will I get in touch with you, Nick?"

"I'm going home to get my gun. Also, call the firehouse and ask around for Carter. He had his suit on this morning, so I don't know where he was going. But tell him what I'm doing. Under no circumstances are you to leave a message with anyone about any of this, got it?"

"Sure, Nick. You sure are fired up."

"I'm pretty sure the reason why Janet was murdered is in her house. I just hope I get to it before anyone else does. One other... no... two other things."

"What's that, Nick?"

"Call Mike and tell him what I'm doing. Do that first. Then call him back with the address as soon as you have it. And, if you track down Carter in time, give it to him as well. I want as many people as possible to know what I'm doing. And here's the last thing."

"What's that?"

"Do not tell my father, under any circumstances, anything about anything. Got that? If he calls, I'm not in. You haven't seen me. You don't know nothin'."

"Got it. Be careful, Nick."

"I'm sure I'm worrying about nothing, but just in case..."

I gave her a quick peck on the cheek and then I was out of there. I flew down the stairs and jumped into the Buick and was off.

...

When I got home, I found my gun and holster and strapped them on under my right arm. I called Marnie and was happy I did.

"I got it, Nick. No problem. The lady at the hospital was real sweet. Tell me when you're ready for the address."

I had a pencil and pad by the phone. When she told

me, I whistled. "I know Nick, right?"

I said, "Twenty thousand bucks can buy a lot of house in this town."

"Wow, Nick."

"Remember. Tell Mike and Carter as soon as you can. Don't tell my father. Got it?"

"Got it."

"You're a doll." I dropped the receiver and ran out the door.

As I drove up Stanyan and passed St. Mary's where I'd last seen Janet, I could feel some of the sadness come back. I'd been doing pretty good since Monday, laying low and nursing the hurt. But this was like re-opening the wound.

The Buick took the hills pretty well. Soon I was over by the Presidio. Janet's house was on Pacific, near Walnut, and it backed up against the Army reservation that had some of the best views in The City.

The house was a newer one. It was covered in shingles, which was smart this close to the ocean. It was two stories, built in a style I'd heard referred to as "organic", but I figured that just meant it was built however the architect wanted.

There was a bank of windows facing west, which I guessed got a pretty great sunset. I went up to the door and tried it. It was locked. But that never really stopped me and, as far as I knew, I was in Janet's will as next of kin, so who was to say I didn't have a right to be here?

I was surprised when I walked in. The house was basically empty. There was a dining table with one chair. A sofa was near the fireplace in the living room, which overlooked a small garden. There was a radio on the mantel. The house was quiet. If anyone had been there, they were gone.

I tried to imagine where Janet would keep important

papers and things like a will or, hopefully, letters that started off, "Here's the answers to all your questions." Those were always helpful, but it had been my experience that they only existed in an author's fevered imagination. In real life, you had little crumbs to follow and, if you were real lucky, they led somewhere. If you weren't, you sometimes fell into traps or got stuck in quicksand. I was hoping neither would be the case here, but I could sense that I was getting close to quicksand.

I walked up the stairs to the second floor and found the one occupied bedroom. It was a brightly lit room in the midday sun. The floor was a blonde wood and the walls were all painted a bright white. There was a double bed in the middle of the room that looked like it hadn't been made up in years.

The room, of course, was a mess, which didn't surprise me at all. Janet had never been able to keep a room clean. This had led to some of the worst of the things that had gone down in our rough and tumble childhood. We looked like the perfect family to most anyone who didn't know us well, but it was basically a living hell that you could only hope to escape from.

I started poking around the room, pulling open drawers and looking through the one bookshelf she had standing against the long wall. Some of the books I recognized from long ago. Then there were the ones she'd probably picked up at Stanford.

A fake treasure chest sitting one of the shelves caught my attention. This would be just the thing to hide important documents in and it would have been something she would have thought very funny.

Janet had a wonderfully weird sense of humor, like the one time she held a trial for one of her dolls and had set up a courtroom, including a jury box of 12 hand-picked dolls. Unfortunately, that one doll was unable to prove its innocence.

She'd asked me to help build a little guillotine but I'd been shocked and appalled and suggested an electric chair instead. So we executed the doll by flipping the lights on and off and making sizzling noises like we'd seen in the movies.

I opened the chest. It was made of wood, cheap wood, actually. And it had bright rhinestone jewels on the lid. There were bits and pieces of actual jewelry inside. Some of it was quite nice. I pocketed the better pieces, thinking I might find someone who would like them. I knew it wasn't necessarily legal but they would be mine to give away if things went well, and if they didn't then no one else deserved to have them.

I looked at the box from the outside more closely and realized there was a false bottom. I looked inside again and, sure enough, there was a little fabric tab hidden underneath a small shelf. I pulled on that and there they were: a couple of letters postmarked from Boston and two official documents of some sort. I grabbed them, stuck them in my coat breast pocket, and then put the box back together and replaced it on the bookshelf.

I looked around and vowed I would be back. I would be back and I would make this a beautiful house and then give it to someone who needed it. There was no reason for it to sit lonely and unloved like this. Poor Janet. She just never learned how to be good to herself.

Chapter 12

3250 Pacific Avenue
Friday, May 15, 1953
About half past 2 in the afternoon

I was going down the stairs when I heard the front door open. I stopped and pressed myself against the wall. Very slowly, I reached in under my left arm and unsnapped my holster. I quietly pulled out the gun. I held it down at my side and softly released the safety.

Maybe it was Mike or Carter, but they would have called out. They wouldn't be sneaking inside.

I thought my best bet was to hide in one of the empty rooms upstairs. I heard whoever it was making noise, like they were opening kitchen drawers. I slowly backed up the steps and then backed into the room right at the top of the stairs. I hid behind the door so I could see out the crack between the door and the frame. I left the door open enough to make sure it was clear that it was an empty room.

I stood there for what seemed like a long time. Whoever was downstairs was still banging around. Then footsteps. I now knew it was a woman. I could hear the distinctive click of heels on the wood stairs. As her head came around the corner, I realized I had no idea who I was seeing. She was moving slowly but with determination, as if it was painful to walk.

Finally, when she got to the top of the stairs, she stopped to take a breath. Then I heard her say, "It's got to be in the bedroom."

I was shocked. It was Marlene, my father's private secretary. I wondered what she was doing here and if she even knew what to look for.

Then I heard another voice. "What do you see?" It was a male voice and definitely not my father's.

"I'm trying the bitch's bedroom."

OK, that pissed me off. I'll admit that none of us Williamses are very lovable but that was a bit much.

Up the stairs came a big, stocky guy. He had dark hair and was wearing a shirt that said, "McAlister Buick." And his name was Marty.

Oh, ho. So, that's how you get a professionally cut brake line and a transmission that keeps going until it hits a brick wall.

Old man McAlister, who was someone I remembered from childhood, was going to have a real fit. This was definitely not good for business.

I listened as they began to tear the room apart. I tried to decide whether to corner them or to let them think they were alone. I figured I had enough pieces to hand Mike for an arrest. But there were two of them and, for all I knew, one or both might be armed.

Considering the way she was walking up the stairs, I could tell she wasn't much of a threat. But there were two kinds of stocky guys in the world: the ones who'd always been fat and had no staying power and the ones who drank too much beer and could always pack a wallop if provoked. I couldn't tell which of these Marty was, so I waited.

Pretty soon they'd gone through the bedroom and the bathroom. He asked, "What about those other rooms?"

"They're all empty. Who buys a brand-new house for cash and then doesn't furnish it?"

In my mind, I answered, "*A woman who was taught to worship at the temple of material success during the height of the Depression when we saw men going hungry outside our house and were told not to help them or give them food or money. A woman who had the guts to go out on her own and try to make something of herself. A woman who, when presented with a shitload of cash, couldn't bring herself to spend any of it. That's who.*"

And then I remembered the car, that flashy, all-new Buick Skylark convertible. And I said to Janet, "Good for you, honey. I hope you drove up and down the coast with the top down and the wind in your hair. I hope you went down to the ocean and swam and I hope you went to wild parties in North Beach. I hope you lived before you died."

Then I had a sickening thought. It was that car that was her demise. This Marty and this Marlene... Two Ms. How cute. These two figured out she had money when she walked in and plunked down six grand all at once.

Since Janet had no sense of how to spend large amounts of money, I imagined she just withdrew the cash at the bank, put it in her purse, probably took the streetcar, for pity's sake, and walked right in, waving 60 hundreds in the air. Just like that.

I wondered when Marlene had come to work for my father and what that connection was. Maybe she had worked at the dealership. Maybe she'd been working for my father for years and it was just a fluke that her employer's estranged daughter should show up where Marty worked and he came home one night and said, "Honey, you won't believe what happened today. All the boys were cracking up about it." Maybe Marlene put two and two together and here we were.

They both went downstairs and slammed the door behind them. I put the safety back on the gun, inserted it into the holster, and strapped it in.

I was sweating in the closed room. I waited about five minutes, just to make sure, and then ran down the stairs and out into the sunshine and fresh air and ocean breezes.

I drove over the hills, fast as I felt I could get away with, to the North District Station. I pulled into the parking lot next to the old, dilapidated building, hopped out of the car, and walked in.

It was the usual afternoon chaos. There were a handful of miserable looking people sitting on the hard wood chairs outside the main room. Phones were ringing and someone was shouting, "Hey! Hey! Anyone hear me?" from somewhere in the back.

I walked up to the desk and asked for Mike. The desk sergeant winked at me and picked up the phone. I wondered what that was about. He spoke down the line, listened, and then said, "Have a seat and the lieutenant will be right out." He smiled real big. It was a come-on if I'd ever seen one. I smiled back, politely, and stood against the wall.

In about two minutes, Mike came tearing around the corner. "Come on. You got your car?"

I followed him. "Sure. What's up?"

He pushed through the door and out into the afternoon sunshine. "Just got a call about your dad's house. Seems like there's a disturbance going on there."

Chapter 13

North District Station
Friday, May 15, 1953
After 3 in the afternoon

I threw him the keys. "You drive. You've got a badge." He caught them and jumped in. It was odd sitting in the passenger seat. I didn't have time to admire the view because Mike was gunning the engine. I grabbed on to the door handle and held on as he squealed out of the parking lot.

We were zooming along and I told him what I'd found.

His only comment was, "Breaking and entering?"

"I'm a family member." I didn't mention the jewelry, but I did mention the papers.

"Have you looked at them yet?"

"No. I wanted to see you first."

"So, you think this Marty guy made your sister and all her cash as a mark and then somehow this Marlene got involved?"

"That's what I'm thinking. I don't know when she started working for my father. I have a theory, but that ain't worth nothin'. You know, until Monday, I hadn't talked to him in over five years."

Mike stopped talking and focused on driving. A motorcycle cop caught us on Van Ness and turned his siren on. Mike waved his badge out the window and then made a series of hand signals. I'd never seen anything like it, but the cop turned off his siren and followed us.

When we got to the top of Nob Hill, we went up Sacramento to the old family house. It sat at the corner of Taylor, across the street from Huntington Park. It was a massive pile of stone that was dated but sturdy.

Mike pulled over in front of the house. He went back to the motorcycle cop and relayed instructions. I guessed he was calling for backup. Mike came back to me and asked, "You have your gun?"

I nodded.

"Is your license current?"

I nodded again.

"Good. You're deputized. Let's go."

He pulled out his revolver and I did the same.

The door was slightly ajar when we got to the top of the stairs. Mike opened the door slowly with the end of his gun. I stood behind him.

I could hear voices. The main hall was two stories high. A staircase led up to the second floor and it was on our left. The hall then emptied into the first sitting room, which was dark. My father's office was the first room on the right from the hall. And that's where the voices were coming from.

I heard a crash and then Marty said, "Old man, I'm losing patience with you. Where is the dough?"

I heard my father's reply. "And I am telling you for the last time, there is no money in this house."

Now that was a lie. A useful lie. A lifesaving lie, most likely. Unless something terrible had happened to the family fortune, Marty was probably standing on top of about two million dollars in gold, cash, and bearer bonds. Janet and I had called it "the mountain." When you opened the safe, that's what it looked like inside. A mountain of all sorts of goodies. But it was almost impossible to detect where in the floor it was hidden. Besides, they would be standing on a massive Persian carpet that had been woven specifically to fit that room.

Mike pointed his head at the room and then quietly said, "On the count of three."

I nodded. I could feel someone behind me. It was the motorcycle cop, who also had his gun drawn. I stepped out of his way, so he could follow Mike. Let the professionals do their job is always my motto.

Marlene was now screeching in a most unfeminine way. "I know you have the loot here, Bobby."

I almost laughed. My father's name was Parnell Robert Williams. I'd never in my life heard or would have ever imagined hearing anyone call him Bobby. Ever.

My father said, "After all I've done for you, Marlene. I was going to propose." Another first. My father sounded betrayed. Usually he skipped betrayal and went straight for bitter anger.

Mike counted softly to three. Then he and the cop moved forward into the doorway of the study.

Mike yelled, "Hold it right there."

"Hey!" was the intelligent reply Marty offered.

I pointed my gun down and waited. Mike said, "You and you. Get on the floor, face down, and put your hands out where I can see them."

There was a pause. The other cop said, "Mister, I

advise you to follow the lieutenant's orders."

Nothing happened.

Then, suddenly, two shots exploded. I heard a thud and Marlene screamed, "You killed him. You bastard, you killed him!"

I ran to the door and was shocked by what I saw. Parnell Robert Williams was holding a smoking gun and still pointing it at Marty, who was lying face up, his unseeing eyes looking at the intricately carved ceiling that was installed way back when.

Mike said, "Drop the gun, Dr. Williams. Just put it down real slow and easy."

My father complied and, as he stood, saw me standing behind Mike. His face was contorted in an emotion I'd never seen him show before. He was sad. He was actually crying. He ran over to me and fell into my arms. "He killed my baby. He killed my baby."

I was baffled, shocked, and felt an odd emotion that I think is called compassion. I awkwardly hugged my father and said something utterly surprising. "That's OK, Daddy. You did what you had to do." That made him cry even harder. I looked around, in a daze, and saw Mike motionless with surprise. Even the motorcycle cop was stunned.

I looked over at Marlene who was standing in the middle of the room. She bent over Marty and started smoothing out his hair.

...

I stood there holding my father and wondering what to do next. Suddenly, I heard very familiar footsteps in the hall and a voice that said, "Dr. Williams? Are you OK?" It was Zelda. The miraculous housekeeper who, in all the years she had worked there, had stayed out of all the family business. She never complained, she never gossiped. She was amazing. I was always in awe of her ability to take care of the most miserable people God ever saw fit to put on this green earth.

She took him out of my arms and led him upstairs. I watched a very old man and a woman, not much younger than him, walk up slowly together. It suddenly occurred to me that Zelda needed to be the next Mrs. Williams. But that was ridiculous. She was too good of a person to ever be a Williams.

I looked at Mike who was now writing something in his notebook. "Are you going to arrest him?" I asked.

"What I am going to do, Nick, is call my captain. Now it's his turn." He smiled a little smile at me and began to walk towards the office phone.

The motorcycle cop was arresting Marlene. He asked, "Should I wait for the squad car, Lieutenant?"

Mike stopped next to me and said, "Yes. I'm about to call down there. Secure the prisoner in one of those chairs. Make sure you take down anything she says. Anything."

I said, "Marlene, I'm not a lawyer, but don't say anything."

She looked up at me with a surprised look and just nodded.

I heard the cop mutter, "Amateurs."

Mike leaned in and whispered to me, "You have a date tonight. When I need your statement, I'll call you. Now get out of here before my captain arrives. Go! Vamoose!"

I nodded and pulled on his arm. "Mike. Thanks."

He just smiled and put his hand on my face. "You'll be fine, kid. Talk to you soon."

I nodded and slipped out the door. I stood in the

front hall and looked around this ghost of a house and could hear so many sounds from long ago, but mostly I could hear Janet laughing like she did before she knew that laughter was not allowed in that house.

Chapter 14

137 Hartford Street
Friday, May 15, 1953
A quarter after 6 in the evening

Somehow, we were ready to go at 6:15. I don't know how we did it. But we got it together.

When I walked in the door, Carter was waiting in the living room. I said, "We know who killed Janet." I fell into his arms and cried for about a minute. That was all I could do.

We walked upstairs together. He used me instead of his cane, which was nice and comforting.

Once we were showered and dressed, I asked, "Should I call Marnie?"

"No. I'll call Marnie. You go down and get the car ready."

I nodded and went outside then realized I had no idea what he meant. I looked at the car. It looked fine. Then I thought about Twin Peaks.

I pulled back the driver's seat to see if there was any trash back there. I found a pop bottle from some unknown source. And a piece of paper. Suddenly, I realized I never looked at the papers I'd found at Janet's house.

I looked up the stairs to see Carter coming out the door. He looked magnificent. He was wearing a new suit. It was perfectly cut for him. I sighed and decided that those papers could wait.

I got in the car and started the ignition. I patted the dashboard and said, "Thanks, baby, for driving so fast today. We'll take it slow tonight."

Carter got in the other side and asked, "Who are you talking to?"

"The car. I was thanking it for driving 70 up Van Ness today."

Carter whistled. "Why don't you tell me about it while we drive up there?"

It was only then that I realized that we were going back to Nob Hill. Everything in the City seemed to revolve around the intersection of California and Mason. It was the crossing of those two particular cable car lines. It's where the Fairmont reigned as princess to the queenliness of the Mark Hopkins. Or maybe that was the kingliness, since it had a masculine name.

As we drove up Market to Van Ness, I told Carter everything. By the time we were making a right on California, I was to the part where my father shot Marty. Carter was impressed. Then I told him the part after that and he was stunned.

"He cried? You called him Daddy?"

"I know. It's amazing, isn't it?"

We were behind a cable car and it stopped to pick up passengers. I just waited. I loved to follow cable cars up California Street. They looked so improbable and yet perfectly formed. They were the heart of San Francisco, moving up and down hills that were too steep for anything else. And everyone loved them. Everyone who wasn't in a hurry that is, as was demonstrated by the honking Fairlane behind me who kept thinking that, if he honked long and hard, then the cable underground would move faster. It didn't.

. . .

We left the car with the keys in it and I handed the kid a five and asked, "Can you keep it ready? We'll be about an hour and a half, I think." He looked at the five and smiled broadly. "Sure thing, mister!"

I remembered the hundred I owed Marcel. And I didn't have it with me. As the doorman opened the door for us, I asked Carter, "Could you loan me a hundred bucks, big guy?"

I knew he kept two of the big bills in his wallet at all times.

"Ooh! Big spender. Whacha buyin'?"

"What I am buying is the best table at the Top of the Mark. A table, I might add, that my vast wealth and notable charm stole from one Mr. George Hearst and his charming wife, Collette, and one Mr. Randolph Hearst and his equally charming wife, Catherine."

"Sweet justice."

"Yes, indeed. Now hand over the dough. Otherwise we'll be eating with the staff, which I'm sure would be fun but wouldn't get the job done here."

Carter reached into his wallet and handed me one of his big bills. It was nicely folded and warm from being against his handsome body.

"What is the job tonight, Nick?"

"At first, it was to shake down Ben White and find out how he arranged getting Taylor Wells all that special treatment Sunday night."

"But now?" Carter was scanning the crowded lobby.

"Now I'm feeling much more generous. Let's see if we can just get these two hitched. How about that?"

"That's fine. Just fine."

Martinelli saw us and waved. He was a bit taller than me and had wonderfully classical Italian good looks. He had thick, wavy, dark hair, black eyes, big, sensual lips, and an easy smile. He obviously was following the same physical plan as Carter because he was covered in muscles. He also must have known a good tailor because he looked like a million bucks in the suit he was wearing. I particularly liked the dark amethyst tie he'd chosen. It was a perfect match to his light olive skin and dark eyes.

"Hi Nick. Good to see you." He shook my hand firmly.

I smiled and said, "Thanks for joining us tonight." Suddenly I realized I didn't know his first name.

I looked up at Carter who was grinning at me. "Carlo."

Martinelli said, "Or Carl. Either one's fine."

I nodded and said, "Carlo. Good to see you again."

He and Carter shook. I looked at my watch. It was five minutes until seven.

I said, "Let's go up. We're gonna to meet Ben at the bar."

The elevator operator was a smartly-dressed woman. She had on a bright red uniform with bright brass buttons. This was topped with a red, square cap.

The three of us were the only ones in the car. She looked over at us and said, "Top of the Mark, of course."

We laughed and Carter said, "Good guess."

She looked at us shrewdly. "So, which two are the couple and which is the blind date?"

We all laughed again. "Psychic?" I asked.

"Nope. Just been doing this a while." She looked at Martinelli and said, "You must be the one the other two are fixing up. And I think I know who you're here to meet." The door opened.

She said, "That blond man, with the martini. That's him, I bet."

I handed her one of the folded fives I had remembered and said, "Thanks. We didn't know what he looked like. Perfect."

She took the five and tipped her red hat at me. "Enjoy the show!"

We stepped into the bar. I walked over to the blond man and asked, "Are you Ben?"

He looked up. He was lean. Probably a couple inches shorter than me. His blond hair was thinning on top but it looked premature. He was probably 30. He had freckles, a big smile, and a warm face. His blue eyes sparkled under the dim lights above the bar.

He extended his hand. "I am. Are you Nick?"

I nodded and said, "Pleased to meet you." I turned and saw that Carter and Martinelli were behind me.

"This is Carter Jones, my friend."

Carter and Ben shook. "And this is Carlo Martinelli, who works with Carter down at the firehouse."

OK, kids. I've seen fireworks. I certainly felt them when I first met Carter. That song, "Some Enchanted Evening." That's our song. That's what happened.

Well, I just watched, absolutely happy for the first time in days, and enjoyed seeing the fireworks on display right there, high above San Francisco.

Carlo settled in at the bar. Ben asked him what he wanted. Carlo couldn't speak. Ben laughed. "He'll have a martini, dry. One olive." Carlo nodded. Ben smiled. It was glorious.

I turned to Carter. "I need to talk to Marcel. Be right back."

I found the marvelous Marcel and he looked quite delighted to see me. I discreetly handed him the folded bill I'd scammed off my husband. He said, "Your table is ready now, Mr. Williams."

I nodded and looked around. "Is the Hearst party here?" Marcel looked a little sheepish. "They will be at the table beside you. That was the best I could do."

I smiled and said, "You have no idea how perfect that is. Thanks again, Marcel."

We sat down, ordered our food, and settled in. The view was glorious. The sunset was on the other side, but we had the Bay Bridge view, which was my favorite.

Carter and I sat next to each other and Carlo and Ben sat on the other side. As we ate, I kept giving the Hearst party sly glances. They were not happy about their table being occupied by us. When they sat down, about ten minutes after we did, they all looked sour.

After about twenty minutes, the elder brother said, "I really wish the City would run all these faggots out of town. San Francisco is too beautiful a place to be ruined by their kind."

His wife put her hand on his arm and said something I couldn't hear.

I looked at Ben who shook his head. I looked at Carlo who nodded. I turned to Carter who also nodded.

I said to Ben, "You're outnumbered. But this has to be a unanimous decision, kid. What do you say?"

He looked around the table. The Hearsts seemed to know what was going on because they got quiet too.

He looked at me and said, "You're the host. You decide."

I put down my napkin and turned to the elder Hearst brother.

"Excuse me, Mr. Hearst?"

He put down his spoon and said, "Yes?"

"You may not remember me, but we met several years ago at your youngest sister's coming out. My name is—"

He screwed up his face and said, "Oh, I know who you are."

His wife said, "George. Be polite."

"I don't mean to be rude or interrupt your meal, but since you've been rude to me, just now, knowing who I am and that your statement was just directed at me, let me tell you this."

I took a deep breath.

"I wouldn't buy a single issue of that rag you call a newspaper, not even to line the cat's tray. You are a blight upon the City and I hope you might have the common decency to leave well enough alone and just report the actual news for a change."

George smirked at me. "I assume you're referring to Monday morning paper?"

"You're damn right I am. You ruined the lives of twenty people. And I bet it didn't improve your circulation one bit because everyone in this town knows what a piece of trash that rag is."

I was getting wrought up now. Carter put his hand on my left arm.

"Young man, you are an offense to all that this City stands for."

"Are you kidding me? This is the Mark Hopkins Hotel, after all, named after a man who killed thousands of coolies to build a railroad. And we're down the street from Huntington Park, named after one of the worst rascals in American history. This City was built on dirty, filthy miners, brothels, lying, cheating, gambling, and everything else you could get down at the Barbary Coast. So don't talk to me about some lofty sentiment about the noble pride of this City. It's been a whore since it was born and it will likely always be one, no matter how pretty it's tarted up to look. And that's what I love about it. It's honest not phony, like you and your paper."

I stood up and said to my friends, "I'm sorry, gentlemen. I'll be at the bar."

I nodded to the ladies at their table. I heard a buzz of chatter in the restaurant as I walked through and took a seat at the bar.

I sat down and said, "Shot of dark rum, please."

It had been a hell of a day, and this was not the end I'd been expecting. But then I looked up and saw Carter leaning on the bar next to me. He was smiling that sweet Georgia smile. "God, I love it when you get on your soapbox. I just wanna..." He leaned over and kissed me right on the mouth. At the Top of the Mark, in front of the children of William Randolph Hearst, and in view of the most magical city on Earth.

Chapter 15

The Top of the Mark
Friday, May 15, 1953
Later that evening

I paid up using my newly minted Diners' Club card. It took a while for the waiter to figure out how to write out the receipt. But we got it handled and then loaded ourselves into the elevator car.

We had the same operator going down that we had coming up. She smiled and looked at Ben. "So, how was the first date?"

He was startled at first and then he shyly took Carlo's hand. "Good. Really good."

She looked at me and said, "I heard that you kicked that idiot Hearst right in the pants."

Carter took my hand and said, "It was magnificent."

The door opened and flashes went off in our faces. I said, "Oh, shit."

We moved out of the elevator and tried to squeeze

through on our way to the door but the small crowd was insistent.

"Mr. Williams? Did you really throw a drink in George Hearst's face?"

I knew this guy was from the *Chronicle*. "No. I just told him what I thought of his paper."

The reporter smiled at me and gave me a thumbs up sign.

Another person asked, "Why were you here tonight?"

I replied, "This has been a very tragic week for my family. I wanted to spend the night with friends having a relaxed dinner."

"Who are your friends?"

"They're just friends."

"Is it true that you and Carter Jones are male lovers and that you live together?"

I was appalled, actually. This was getting out of hand. I turned to Carter who just shrugged and then pulled me into a side hug. The cameras went off.

"We do live together. We are very good friends."

"How is your father?"

"He's resting. Today was a very trying day."

"Will you be speaking at your sister's memorial tomorrow?"

I actually didn't know the answer to that question. "I don't know the exact program but I can tell you that I miss my sister. She was one hell of a gal."

More cameras exploded.

"Are you still the wealthiest man in San Francisco?"

"I don't know. You'll have to ask Bank of America. They handle all my money. And quite well, in fact. Everyone should bank with them."

There were some laughs when I said that.

"OK, fellas. One last question."

"Who killed your sister?"

"Ask the police."

I grabbed Carter's hand and we pushed through the scrum with Ben and Carlo behind.

The car was right where I'd left it. The kid was standing there, the engine was running, and we all piled in. I handed him my last five and said, "Thanks, kid."

He saluted me and said, "Thank you, Mr. Williams. I hate the *Examiner*!"

I smiled at him and then pulled the Buick around the brick drive as the cameras followed us, taking more photos. We moved out onto California Street heading west.

Carter said, "You were magnificent back there."

Carlo said, "Yeah. That was really something." He sounded doubtful. I didn't blame him. He signed up for a date, not a blinding journalistic frenzy.

I looked at the two lovebirds through the rear-view mirror. They were holding hands. At least the date part was going well.

I took Carter's hand and held it. It was a double date, after all.

. . .

We went up to the top of Twin Peaks. It's the best Lover's Lane in all these United States. What better place to go? No streetlights. No cops. Just an amazing view of our very own Baghdad by the Bay.

After about thirty minutes of serious necking, in the front seat and in the back, we all decided to head home.

Carlo gave me his address. He wasn't far from us. His apartment was in a building across from Dolores Park. We pulled up and I looked in the mirror again. Ben was nodding as if he was saying yes to an invitation. They both slid out.

Carlo said, "Thanks for an amazing evening, Carter." He paused. "Nick."

Ben leaned down and looked at me through Carter's window. "Thanks, Mr. Williams. I'll never forget tonight."

I laughed and said, "My pleasure. I expect you won't forget this evening for a very long time. Our picture will probably be on the front page of every paper tomorrow morning."

Carter added, "Except the *Examiner*."

Ben turned white, which was quite a feat for him, considering how pale he was already. "Do you think so?"

I nodded. "Will that hurt you at work?"

He looked scared and nodded. "It might."

"Well, tell you what. You call me if anyone gives you grief. You two go have a good night and don't worry about any of this. We'll get it all sorted out. I have great lawyers. Now, scoot you two!"

They both waved and ran up the steps to Carlo's apartment.

We drove home slowly. I enjoyed holding Carter's hand in the car. Something had happened that night. It wasn't just the satisfaction of calling out George Hearst, although that was fun. Something else had changed. And, as smart as I thought I was, I couldn't put my finger on it.

We pulled up into the driveway and parked the car.

Mike was standing, once again, under the porch light, reading yet another dime-store novel and smoking the stub of yet another cigar.

Carter and I hobbled and walked up the steps.

Carter said, "Mike."

"Carter."

"You alone?"

"Yep. Looks like you are, too."

I shook my head and, pushing through the two behemoths, opened the door. I was glad to be home and wondering why Mike was there.

"Is Nick around?" Mike was continuing their little game.

Carter pushed the door closed behind him, pulled me into his arms, and said, "Yeah. He's right here. And I'm so proud of him, I could burst."

"Yeah, well that's, um, why I'm here, actually." I suddenly realized he'd been showing a false bravado out on the porch. He looked sad and upset.

"What's up, Mike?"

"Well, before we get to that. Marlene confessed."

I nodded.

"Marty knew from the sales guy about your sister waving around a lot of cash at McAlister's. He told Marlene and she put it together that this was your sister. She knew your old man had a big stash under the floor and figured Janet would have the same."

I looked at Carter who nodded.

"Pure coincidence then. So, why did they go after Janet first?"

"Easier mark, from what I could tell."

"Yeah. That safe in my father's house is hard to get into. Besides, breaking the combination and figuring out how to open the floor up, the rug has to be taken up in a very specific way."

He nodded. "The opportunity came when she took the car in on Monday for service. Marty bumped another mechanic. Said he was a friend of the family and wanted to make sure it was done right."

I rolled my eyes and turned to look out the dark window.

Mike continued. "He must have cut the lines in a way so that it wouldn't be immediately obvious. She might have been driving around for a while before that happened. As for the transmission, she probably just thought the car was running rough."

"Old man McAlister is gonna be very upset that a murder was planned in his own garage."

Mike laughed bitterly and said, "Yeah. We already talked to him. He took it badly."

I looked at Mike. It was obvious that he was hurting bad and it didn't have anything to do with Janet, Marlene, my father or old man McAlister.

"What else is it, Mike?"

"Your little set-to at the Mark Hopkins?"

I said, "Yeah. What about that?"

"The mayor, the goddam mayor, 'Rob-Rob' himself, called me personally thirty minutes ago and wanted to know if it was true that I was your friend. He wanted to know how well I knew you. Asked me all sorts of questions."

"What did you say?"

"I told him the truth."

Carter whistled. "What happened?"

"Suspended. No pay. Indefinite."

I was incensed. "What? Are you kidding me?"

"Nope. There's more."

"Oh shit."

"Ben White. Suspended indefinitely without pay. Carlo Martinelli. Suspended indefinitely without pay. Carter Jones. Fired."

Carter moved to the sofa and collapsed. I said, "I need a goddam drink."

The phone rang. I said, "Someone else answer it if you want to. I'm not up to it right now. Who wants what?"

The phone kept ringing.

Mike said, "Rye, neat."

Carter didn't reply. I asked him again. No reply. The phone kept ringing. I walked over to it, lifted up the receiver, and dropped it down again. I counted to five and then I took the receiver off and laid it down on the shelf.

I looked into the living room. Carter was just staring into space. Mike was standing, chewing on his cigar, but it had gone out. I poured Mike his drink and took it to him.

I leaned down next to Carter and said, "Honey, talk to me."

He looked at me blankly. "That's all I ever wanted to do. All my life. And to work in this city, where it means something big, real big, to be a fireman. That's all I ever wanted to do. All my life." His face was hollow. It was distressing to see, to say the least.

I took his hand and I said, "We can go anywhere, we can do anything you want. You know that. We don't have to stay here."

That seemed to shake him. He looked at me, as if noticing I was there for the first time, and said, very quietly, "Hell no. I'm not leavin'. They can fire me, they can call me names, but I'm not leaving. This is my home. I live here with you, my husband." He reached over and pulled me in for a deep and probing kiss.

When he released me, I fell back and said, "Whoa."

Mike asked, "Do you want me to leave?"

I said, "Hell, no. No one leaves. Everyone gets drunk. That's an order."

As I stood up to go get myself a drink, I had a thought. "Should we tell Ben and Carlo?"

Mike asked, "How did that go, by the way?"

Carter laughed wryly. "Beautifully. One hell of a way to start a new relationship."

I asked, "What do you guys think?"

Mike said, "I'd want to know. I would hate to find out you knew and didn't tell me." He looked down at Carter. "That's why I came over here to wait for you."

I nodded and said, "You're right." I looked at Carter. "Do you have Carlo's phone number?"

"No, but he should be in Polk's."

I went over to the phone alcove and pulled out the big monster book. I looked up his name, and there he was at the right address. I pressed the switch hook on the phone and held it to get a new line. As I did so, it rang.

I answered it. "Yeah?"

"Nick?"

"Carlo? I was just about to call you."

"Yeah, well, I just heard from my chief. And he, um, he told me about the other guys as well. Um, can you come over? Ben seems to not be taking it very well."

"Why? What's going on?"

"He's lying on my bed, crying. I don't know what to do."

"Hold on. We're coming over."

I put down the phone and looked over at Carter and Mike. "Load 'em up, fellas. We have some queers we need to go rustle up."

Chapter 16

696 Church Street
Friday, May 15, 1953
Much later that evening

When we got to Carlo's apartment, he was sitting outside on the steps, which was probably a good thing since I had neglected to ask for his apartment number.

During the short drive, Carter had said, "Let me handle this." Not only was his soft, southern voice persuasive, I figured I'd made enough trouble all over town today that I didn't need to make things worse in this budding relationship.

I pulled alongside the curb and Carter lifted himself out of the car. He hobbled over and up the steps. Plopping himself down, he began to talk to the poor guy, who looked like he'd just lost his last friend.

Mike said, "This is pretty bad stuff here, Nick."

I turned around in the seat and looked back at him. He was slouched against the corner and looked pretty glum as well.

"How are you handling this, Mike?"

He looked down at his hands and then back up at me. "I'm like Carter. All I've ever wanted to be was a policeman. I can't imagine doing anything else."

I looked at my friend and started thinking. It was the germ of an idea, but the more I thought about it, the more I liked it.

I turned back around and looked up the street and out over the park. The city lights were dim and this was that wonderful time of night when San Francisco sparkled, even in a residential section like this.

Suddenly, I had it. I hit the horn twice and said, "Fuck yeah!"

Mike said, "What the hell, Nick? People are trying to sleep here."

I turned around and said, "I want you to come to work for me, Mike!"

"I ain't no gumshoe. Besides, what about a license? Yours is probably on thin ice as it is."

"We'll sue, then. Come on, Mike, come work for me. You can run the whole outfit. I don't care."

Without waiting for a reply, I jumped out of the car, ran up the steps, and said, "Look, you guys. Stand up. Stop feeling sorry for yourselves."

I pulled Carter up by the arm and said, "Kiss me, you fool. I have an idea!"

He looked at me like I'd just grown a new head, but he did reach down and kiss me softly on the lips.

"Carter Jones, you are an amazing man and I love you."

I looked over at Carlo, who had stood up but was looking at me warily as though I was about to ask for a big smackeroo from him as well.

"Carlo, go get your boyfriend. You're coming home

with us. We have some work to do, kid."

Carlo looked at Carter with a questioning face. Carter replied, in his even drawl, "When the richest man in San Francisco asks to you come over for a meetin', I would suggest you take him up on the invitation, son."

Carlo shrugged and went up the steps. I said, "Pick up your steps, kid. Today is the best day of your life and it ain't over yet!"

. . .

Carlo and Ben piled into the back seat with Mike. We drove back over to the house and it was all I could do not to push each one of these slow pokes up the stairs and in the door.

I said, "The bar is open. Help yourselves. There's beer and pop in the fridge. Take what you want. But don't drown your sorrows because the night ain't over."

They all looked at me and Carter said, "Uh, Nick? What the hell is all this about?"

"We're going to start our own Pinkerton's!"

Mike smiled and said, "You mean you want to hire us as private eyes?"

"No, doofus. I mean we're going into the security business."

Ben asked, "What's the difference?"

"The difference is in the licensing. The difference is in the services. The difference is that ever since the Secret Service started, no one has picked up where Pinkerton's left off."

"But, Nick..."

"No more buts. Everyone get your drinks and your eats and meet back here in ten. I have a phone call to make."

I practically skipped into the hallway, I was so fucking happy. I picked up the phone and listened for the whirr. I dialed Marnie's home number and waited for her to answer.

After about twelve rings, she did and she was sleepy and not happy. "What is it?"

"Marnie, dear. Marnie, sweetheart. Wake up!"

"Nick, what the hell?"

"Look sweetums, this is your lucky day. How fast can you get dressed and over here?"

"Are you at home?" I heard her yawn.

"I sure am. How fast?"

"I dunno. Thirty minutes?"

"Make it twenty."

"Look, Nick. What is this about?"

"It's about a brand-new day. It's about you and me and four other poor old guys starting a whole new life and a new way of doing business. It's about the future and, from where I stand, doll, it's looking bright!"

There was a long pause. "Put Carter on the phone, Nick."

He was hobbling past so I handed him the instrument.

"Hi Marnie. Were you asleep?"

Medium pause.

"No, he's not drunk." He looked at my eyes. "And he's not stoned."

Medium pause.

"How the hell should I know? He's going on about Pinkerton's and the Secret Service and I don't know what the hell else."

Long pause. I pulled his arm. He yanked it back, a little irritated, and I couldn't blame him. He couldn't see what I could see.

"Bring her along. She can sleep in one of the guest bedrooms."

Short pause.

"No, I'm sure. I'll call a cab for you. No, Nick will. But we'll see you in a minute. Bye, Marnie."

He put the receiver down.

"I hope you know what you're doing. You're getting a 62-year-old woman out of her beauty sleep and she won't be happy."

I stood up on my toes and gave Carter a long, passionate kiss.

"Hey. What's that for?"

"For being you. And for the future."

...

We worked through dawn. Once Marnie arrived, and Carter had tucked her mother into bed, complete with a hot toddy, we all sat down and I explained my idea.

At first, there was a whole chorus of "what ifs," and "yeah, buts," and that was fine. I was willing to sit with these wonderful folks and talk about this idea until I ran out of words.

I knew that this was a great idea and that these were the perfect 5 business partners to get it off the ground.

Carlo and Ben, being the youngest members of our group, were the least adventurous, for some reason.

Finally Mike, who was now on board and seemed to get the idea even better than me, sat down in front of them both and said, bluntly, "The worst that can happen is you'll make a lot of money sitting on your ass. That's the worst, fellas. And, considering you will never, ever be hired to work in this country again as either a cop or as a fireman, because you're both known to be practicing queers, this is the sweetest deal you've got."

Around 5:30, they both came around and we were all in. And that felt good.

About 6:15, Marnie and I went into the kitchen to put

on another pot of coffee. I looked in the icebox and realized we had no food to speak of.

I decided it was time for us to either shut it down and pick up on Monday or keep going, but out at an early-morning diner. But even my eyes were drooping. Marnie was yawning while filling the percolator.

I said, "Forget that. Why don't you stay here and get some sleep? I'll take Carlo and Ben home. Mike can bunk on the couch."

Marnie said, "Thanks, Nick. I really don't want to wake up Mother again."

I nodded and then realized something very important. Something crucial. Something absolutely necessary.

I said, "You go in and tell the guys the plan. I have to go get something out of the basement."

She looked at me funny but then said, "Sure thing, Nick."

As soon as she was gone, I ran around to the basement door and down the stairs, taking them two steps at a time.

I had my own mountain. After living with so much cash and what-not hidden in the house when I was growing up, it only made sense to do the same here. Only Carter knew about the safe and how it worked. We'd fixed it so that different guys worked on different parts of putting it together. That way no one person, other than us two, knew that it was here or how to work it.

I walked around behind the washing machine that was mostly for show, since we sent out our laundry, and pulled very gently on the little string that looked like it was stuck on the wall.

Doing this activated a mechanism that caused a piece of the concrete wall to the right to start moving. It was quiet as a whisper in church. You could barely tell it was opening just by looking at it.

Once the wall was open, this revealed a combination safe, which I opened in a jiff.

My mountain was nowhere near two million dollars like my old man's, but it was plenty. I took out a bank-wrapped bundle of hundreds from one stack of several and divvied it up into five equal parts. I rolled these smaller stacks of two grand each and wrapped them like the gangsters do. I thought that gave it all a nice touch.

I pushed the safe door closed and spun the dial for good measure. I gently pushed the outer mechanism closed until I heard a very faint click and then carried the dough upstairs. I grabbed a sack on my way up the stairs and stashed it all in there.

When I walked into the living room, I grinned. Ben was dozing on Carlo's shoulder. Mike was leaning up against the armchair looking up at the ceiling. I could almost see little cartoon drawings of action and adventure popping out of his head as he thought about what all of this meant.

Carter had his leg propped up on the table under a pillow. Marnie was looking out the window at the brightening sky.

"OK, team. One last thing." I held the sack out in front of me and said, "Come and get it. This is the final part, before we sign any papers on Monday, to finish up our first conference."

Carlo nudged Ben, who woke up and looked around and said, "What?"

Mike stood up and then pulled Carlo up off the sofa and Carlo then pulled Ben up. I liked the look of that. Carter grumbled under his breath about getting up but he did. Only Marnie stayed where she was.

"Marnie?"

"Be with you in a minute, Nick."

The other guys came over and stood in front of me. "Whatcha got there, Nick, lollipops?" asked Mike with a wink.

"No, you big ape. Something better. Reach in and take one."

He put his paw in the bag and pulled out one of the rolls. He looked at me and then shook his head.

I said, "No refusals. Each one of you has to take one. Or else you're out."

Mike smiled and said, "Well, this is a nice howdy-doo."

I smiled back and said, "You deserve it. You all deserve it."

By this time Ben and Carlo had taken one each. Ben unbound his and said, "Gosh, Mr. Williams. I've never seen this much cash at one time before."

"The name's Nick, kid."

He looked at me and said, "Well then, Nick. My name's Ben."

I winked at him and nodded.

I pushed the bag towards Carter and said, "You're next, big boy."

He smiled lazily and put in his hand. "Seems like I already have plenty of this stuff, Nick."

I shrugged. "Share and share alike."

"Marnie?" I called out. She was still staring at the window.

She turned around and I saw that her face was wet.

"Gosh, Nick. My whole life's about to change, ain't it?"

I nodded and said, "It sure is, sweetheart. And here's the first installment." I offered her the bag and she took out the last roll.

"Gee Nick. I don't know what to say."
"Say goodnight, Gracie."
"Goodnight, Gracie."
We all laughed.

Chapter 17

137 Hartford Street
Saturday, May 16, 1953
Just past 10 in the morning

Around 10 that Saturday morning, I felt Carter poking me in the ribs.

"Get up, Nick. We have to be at Grace Cathedral at noon."

I said, "Right."

I had only had coffee the night before, so why did I feel hung over?

I put my feet on the floor and lazily walked to the bathroom. Not at all to my surprise, I found a giant standing where I needed to stand. So I turned on the shower to get the hot water heater going. I was going to need a good, hot shower.

I looked in the mirror and then turned away. I was too old to stay up until dawn and too young to be looking like I had stayed up until dawn.

Carter and I switched places. He said, "How are you feeling about your plan there, Nick?"

I said, "Good. A bit more realistic in the cold light of later in the morning but still good. They're the right guys, and gal, and the right idea."

"You know what I liked about it most?" God, I loved listening to this man talk. I would have sat enraptured while he read from Polk's. Seriously.

I moved into the shower and asked, "What?"

"That you really let Mike take the lead once he got the idea."

I nodded and said, "And, let me tell you, that's a relief. When he sat down in front of the Bobbsey Twins—"

"Nick!"

"Yeah, I know. But it's true, ain't it?"

"It is. It is, at that."

"Anyway, when he sat down in front of Ben and Carlo and spelled it out, I knew he was hooked. In the car, when the idea came to me, I told him he could take it and run with it. I'm glad he took me up on that. That was while you were applying whatever healing balms you were applying to Carlo on the steps—"

"I was just telling him to be patient and that everything was going to turn out fine."

Carter really could sell ice to an Eskimo. Personally, I like being sold to by him. Makes me feel all funny and warm inside, like he's my best friend, which he is.

"Was he buying it?"

"Maybe. Then you jumped in and what I'd said didn't matter."

At this point, Carter was behind me, lathering up and, from time to time, rubbing on my shoulders.

I turned around and said, "Carter Jones, you take that back. Take that back right this minute."

He lifted his soapy hands in protest. "What?"

"Everything that comes out of your mouth is pure gold."

He grinned his lazy Georgia grin at me and, once again, we drained the hot water heater. And with guests in the house, no less.

. . .

We both wore black suits. When I got downstairs, Marnie was making toast because toast was all there was to make. Oh, and coffee. Glorious coffee.

"What's this red jam, Nick?"

"That's Mrs. Jones's award-winning red plum jam. It's the only kind that Carter likes and I have to agree with him."

"His mother sends it to him?"

"No. It comes via his aunt, who is the one kind soul in Albany, Georgia, who will give either of us the time of day. I don't know how she does it, but she convinces Carter's mother to make up a huge batch each year for the Confederate Veterans or the local orphans and then she sends a goodly portion of it to us. She's smart that Aunt Velma. She sits on the board of the county hospital and, as if by magic, every year the Dougherty County Hospital Board gets a nice big check from the Williams Benevolent Foundation. I also send her a little something every spring so she can pay her sister-in-law for more Mason jars and to cover postage. I always tell her to insure the package for at least five hundred bucks. Because it's worth it, ain't it?"

She was looking at me sideways. "How much of that is true and how much of that is just good storytelling?"

I slathered some of the very same jam on a piece of toast. "It's all true, my dear. I would never lie about jam."

A little dollop fell on my black pants. Before I could do anything, Marnie had wet the end of a towel under the sink and handed it to me. "Seltzer, my dear. It's the only thing that works on wool." I went over to the bar and squeezed a bit out of the siphon and that did the trick.

I walked back into the kitchen and looked at Marnie. "So, sweetheart, how're you feeling about becoming the Board Secretary of the Whatzit Investigations Amalgamated, Inc.?"

She looked at me dead on and said, "I hope you were serious about all that last night because I haven't told you one important thing 'cause of all the goings and comings and what-not."

"What's that?"

"Mother and me are being evicted."

"What? But I thought you were fine for money."

"Oh, it ain't the money. It's the freeway. The state is taking the building. We just rent, you know. The landlord already got paid. We have 15 days to vacate."

I nodded and asked, "Do you like being by the ocean?"

Marnie looked at me sideways again.

"Yeah, why?"

"Well, I happen to know of a charming spot on Pacific that might need a tenant."

Marnie's eyes widened. "Nick! That's your sister's house!"

"My sister is no longer available to live there, being otherwise occupied."

"What will Mother say?"

"It's way out there, Marnie. There's no streetcar anywhere near to be found."

Marnie nodded and then looked at me. "I was actually thinking of buying a car with the dough you gave me this morning."

"Perfect! It's settled then."

Marnie came over and gave me a hug and a kiss on the cheek.

"Don't kiss me yet, doll. I don't know that the house is mine. Oh shit! Wait right here. Be right back."

I ran up the stairs, into the bedroom, and bumped right into Carter.

"What's the hurry, son?"

"The papers."

"What papers?" He was standing in between me and the bedroom and I got the sense he was enjoying keeping me in my place.

"The ones I found at Janet's house yesterday. I never looked at them."

He moved to the side and let me through. I rifled through yesterday's coat and found them. There were the two letters and the two official documents.

I said to Carter, "Come on. There's toast and coffee downstairs. We need to look at these before I see my father today."

I bounded down the stairs. I then realized Mike was nowhere to be seen. I walked into the kitchen and sat down at the table.

Carter came in behind me and poured himself a cup of coffee. Marnie said, "Good morning, Carter."

He smiled and said, "Good morning, Marnie. Are you invited to this shindig today?"

I looked up and shook my head. "I don't want her to get hurt. It's not going to be pretty. My father is going to be at his absolute worst today. I'm sure he's mortified that he cried in front of me."

Marnie said, "I couldn't go if I wanted. Mother isn't awake yet."

Carter handed Marnie a twenty and said, "For a cab.

You stay as long as you want." He handed her another twenty. "And that's for groceries, unless your mother is dieting."

Marnie giggled. I watched her blithely slip the two bills inro her purse. I really loved that she was so good at receiving money from people. It was a quality I never had to develop because I had an allowance, which was like swallowing glass and quite painful to receive and I had a hard time spending it, until Uncle Sam became my employer that is. And then, all of sudden, at 21, I was suddenly very rich. Even now, the truth was I'd rather live in Eureka Valley than up on Nob Hill, and most of it had to do with not wanting to spend the ill-gotten gains of rakish Uncle Paul.

I turned my attention back to the letters. They were from Uncle Paul, of course. The gist of the first letter was mainly that my father was a dick, although Uncle Paul was much more eloquent than that. It had been sent to Janet for her 21st birthday by Uncle Paul's estate lawyer in Boston. It said that there was a little something enclosed to celebrate an important milestone in a young woman's life. It also suggested not marrying too early. And there were other bits of solid, good advice designed to enlighten and liberate rather than calling for adherence to cultural norms. Good ole Uncle Paul.

The second letter was mailed from Boston as well and the postmark was dated late March of '52. It was longer and it explained that Janet was the beneficiary of a trust similar to mine. For some reason, not explained, she came into the trust at age 25. He may have been a sinner of the Sodom variety, but apparently Uncle Paul still held some old-fashioned ideas about women and property.

The letter went on to suggest very strongly that

Janet draw up a will that excluded everyone but me. Uncle Paul was very specific about this. I'd received similar advice and Jeffery had worked on my will for almost six months to make sure that no Williams, including my own father, would try to kill me so they could inherit.

The letter continued with more of that solid, good advice but contained a little extra something that was amazingly prescient:

"And, for goodness' sake, be sure to go out and live. I know those of you who are living through this Depression are bound to be cautious, thinking that the sky may fall at any moment, like it did on your parents. But, my dear niece, may I assure you that the sky will never fall on your head. So, go out there and grab the apple. Live life and, please, be kind to yourself and the ones you come across. And, for my sake, be nice to your brother. He's a good soul and is walking the same path as myself, which is not always a happy journey. I wish you all the very best with this gift I am so very pleased to make for you. Take it and live long in health, joy, and love."

I handed this letter to Carter, who was munching jammy toast. Marnie, who was the world's best busybody, read it over his shoulder, which was hard to do since he was so much taller than her.

I then pulled out the two official documents. One detailed the terms of the trust. I was familiar with this one. I had one just like it. I scanned the document to see if there was anything different about it, and there wasn't.

I then looked at the second one and it was her will. And, look at that, Jeffery Klein, Esquire, was her attorney. Well, bully for Janet. And bully for Jeffery. I guess all he had to do was get out the boiler plate from mine.

I read through it and was surprised by nothing. The Williams Benevolent Foundation was about to get a whole lot larger.

"Well, Marnie, the house isn't mine to let. But I will make a handsome offer to purchase it from the Williams Benevolent Foundation and I have a feeling they will gladly sell. I think you'll find the rent to be very affordable."

She said, "Thanks, Nick. That's real swell. Mother's going to love living so close to the ocean."

I said, "And think of all those soldiers at the Presidio, just over the hill from you."

Marnie said, "You know I ain't interested in that. I'm going to the market. When do you leave?"

I looked at my watch. It was just right at 11. "In about 15 minutes. Stay as long as you like. Don't rush on our account. By the way, where is Mike?"

Marnie shrugged. "Beats me. He was gone when I came down."

She came over and gave me another peck on the cheek. She looked at Carter and said, "I know he's a pain, but you got a good man there, Carter."

He smiled at her and said, "He is. And I know it. Thanks, Marnie, for coming in on this deal with us."

She waved at both of us and hurried out the front door. I think she was trying not to cry in front of us again.

Carter looked at me and asked, "So, does the foundation get it all?"

I nodded.

"How much?"

"Based on the trust document, the endowment is about to double."

Carter just shook his head. "How did he do it? That's... That's a hell of a lot of money, Nick."

I nodded. "I know. And, truth be told, we really don't want to know how."

He just grinned at me. He had a spot of red plum jam on the corner of his mouth. I had to lick it off, of course. Good jam should never be wasted.

Chapter 18

On the way to Grace Cathedral
Saturday, May 16, 1953
Just before noon

It was one of those perfect San Francisco days. The sky was that kind of blue that you only see in our fair city. Not a cloud anywhere. A nice breeze and a warm May sun.

We took a cab to the cathedral. I had an idea that maybe we could walk down to Grant Street afterward and have some dim sum. I didn't want to have to deal with parking where there wouldn't be any.

I turned to Carter. "I should call Jeffery and let him know all about our new plan."

"He'll show up for the service, won't he?"

I shrugged. "Maybe. I don't know how things are with his new friend."

"Well, you have to take the will to him, right?"

"He already has a copy. That's why I don't know if

we'll see him. He should've already called me, as the sole heir."

I noticed that, as we were talking, the cab driver kept looking in his rear-view mirror at me. I asked him, "So, did we make the front page this morning?"

The guy snapped his fingers and said, "I knew that was you. I fuckin'..." He looked contrite for a moment. "Pardon my language..."

"Have at it, brother," I said.

"I fuckin' hate them Hearsts. Good for you! And, you know, I grew up on a farm. I know the good Lord made everyone in His liking, so you won't get no trouble from me on account of your, uh, proclivities."

This actually shook me a bit. Maybe we should have looked at the paper before venturing out.

"Do you have a copy with you?"

"Sure! It's the *Call-Bulletin*, if you don't mind that."

"And such a venerable newspaper in this City? Of course not."

Carter whispered, "Lay off the high-hat talk," as the man passed the paper over the back of the seat.

I spread it out and we both looked. It wasn't horrible, but it wasn't good.

"Gay Ole Time at the Top of the Mark." That was the main headline. The sub went like this: "Great-nephew of Paul Williams Keeps Family Legacy Alive."

That one made me laugh. Carter was looking at the photo. "You're right. I am a giant. They almost cropped my head off."

I elbowed him. "That's what you're looking at?" I looked over at him and he grinned.

We both turned back to the story. It was written a bit floridly, but that was the way the queer stories always came out. Apparently, I had stood up, both hands on my hips, and spat at the horrified Mr. George Hearst.

Mrs. George Hearst was reportedly terrified, according to witnesses and family friends.

No mention was made of his brother, Randolph, or his lovely sister-in-law, Catherine, which I thought strange. I looked for the byline. Oh, ho. There was none, of course.

I assumed the story in the *Chronicle* would feature the embarrassment to the Hearsts and would skip much of the rest. In this paper, there was a separate story, with a byline, about the mayor's vow to clean the city ranks of any known homosexuals, Communists, and other deviants. Good ole Rob-Rob.

The cab pulled up on Jones at the entrance to the partially-completed cathedral. There was a mob of reporters waiting. I threw the guy his paper, a twenty, and said, "Thanks!"

He replied, "Don't mention it. Good luck with them jackals."

We jumped out and I let Carter, my personal giant, run interference. He pushed his way through and we dashed up the steps and into the safety of the sanctuary.

It was dark inside, as it always was. The stained glass was beautiful, as always. A minister of some sort extended his hand and said, "I'm so sorry for your loss, Mr. Williams." I nodded. He then shook Carter's hand. "And, I'm so sorry for all that has happened in the last day, Mr. Jones." This was nice. Real nice.

"Won't you follow me in here? I wanted to have a few words with you both before we begin."

We followed the minister, or priest, I really had no idea of his title, into a small room. He closed the door behind us and said, "I am the Right Reverend Simon Acre. I am the Bishop of California. I will be performing the memorial service for your sister."

I said, "Thank you..." I paused, not knowing the right word.

"Bishop."

"Thank you, Bishop."

Carter and I were holding our hats in our hands nervously. I felt like we'd been called into the principal's office and were in trouble.

"I wanted to speak with you both briefly before we started. I have two objectives. The first being that I would like to add any particular anecdotal stories about your sister that you would like for me to share. Are there any that come to mind?"

I thought for a moment and then remembered what I'd heard the previous day in that old pile of rocks just a block away.

"Janet was a very happy baby. I loved to listen to her laugh, even when no one was in the room with her. She seemed to think everything was funny back then."

The bishop smiled and nodded. "Anything else?"

I said, "I don't how you'll take this or whether you can use it, but we had a miserable childhood. And it was lousy. But she seemed to take it all in stride. And she was very generous." I thought about the Foundation. "In fact, you can share that her sizable estate has been left absolutely to the Williams Benevolent Foundation."

The bishop smiled again and asked, "Oh, is that a family tradition?"

I said, "Not really. Let's say it's starting with our generation." I remembered one other thing. "You could also say that she got in a lot of trouble every time she tried to sneak bread or fruit or anything, really, to the men who were lined up on California Street, you know."

The bishop shook his head and said, "I know. Why

don't I just say that she was generous to a fault, even as a child?"

I smiled and said, "That's perfect."

The knot in my stomach was growing tighter. I looked at Carter, who was somber, and then at the bishop.

"What was the other thing, Bishop?"

He looked a little pained. "Would you be amenable to sitting only with immediate family?"

I wasn't and wouldn't be but this was Janet's day. I looked at Carter, who shrugged. "This is about your sister, Nick."

The bishop put his hand on Carter's arm and smiled up at him. "Good man."

For some reason, I burst into tears when he did that.

. . .

I sat up on the front pew, quite alone. The cathedral was packed with well-wishers, gossip mavens, curiosity seekers, professional Williams family haters (and there were plenty of these, as they had every right to be), and assorted other types.

Carter was back, a couple of rows behind me. He was seated with Ben, Carlo, and Mike, who had all shown up unannounced but not unwelcome. This show wasn't anything I would wish on an enemy, not to mention a really good friend. Pam and Diane were there, too, seated with them. Pam was wearing the dress she'd worn to our last function together.

My father was nowhere to be seen. Nor were any of his siblings or the assorted cousins, first, second, or third. In fact, it looked like I was the only Williams present because, in the time-honored tradition of our crazy family, Janet's ashes were up on the altar. I guess it was the only safe thing to do. Cremate the bastards just in case they weren't actually dead.

It was ten after and the bishop looked at me from where he was seated. The massive organ was playing some beautiful Bach, which I was very much enjoying. I shrugged and mouthed, "Go ahead."

The Right Reverend Simon Acre, Bishop of California, stood and the organist very quietly brought that particular fugue to an end. He looked across the crowded room and said, "Today we remember the life of Janet Leticia Williams."

At that moment, I heard a sound in the back. There were several people whispering and I could hear people turning in their pews. I turned around and could see only a single man standing in the door to the great cathedral. He was in shadow as the blinding light of the beautiful San Francisco day made it impossible to see anything else.

"Wait! I killed her." It was, of course, my father.

I stood up and began to walk quickly down the aisle. The organ began again. Carter caught up with me and whispered, "Do you think he's drunk?"

I nodded.

"I killed her! I killed my baby!" There were exclamations and furious whispers that were getting louder as we walked along the gangplank to the back of the cathedral.

When we could finally see him, it was obvious that he was drunk. There were journalists outside, snapping up all the juiciness of the latest Williams family scandal.

I said, not kindly, "You're drunk, old man. Come on."

I pulled on him and he pulled away.

"Don't touch me, you faggot."

Carter grabbed the man, who was only 5'8" tall and weighed maybe 130 pounds when wet, and began carrying him towards the small room where we had met with the bishop.

As we walked briskly, my father started howling, "Put me down, you fucking fairy. Let me go!"

I said, "Shut up, old man, or I'm gonna sock you in the face."

That shut him up.

Chapter 19

Grace Cathedral
Saturday, May 16, 1953
A quarter past noon

We got to the room and Carter dropped him unceremoniously on the floor. He sat there, crying. Carter stood with his back to the door. No one was leaving or coming in.

I pulled my father up by his arm and pushed him into one of the wooden chairs that were arranged in a circle.

"Why are you here, old man?" I was mightily pissed but I was also feeling a terrible pity for him. I knew why he was there. He felt guilty. But he felt guilty for all the wrong things, as usual.

"I killed her. Don't you understand? She wouldn't be dead if it weren't for me." He was still sobbing. His suit was a mess. He smelled of vodka, his drink of choice.

I sat down on my haunches and said, "You are an evil bastard but you're no killer."

He looked at me, astonished that I would call him that. "But Marlene—"

"But Marlene, nothing. That was pure circumstance."

He shook his head. "No. No. She came to me begging for a job because she knew—" He started sobbing again.

"She knew what?"

"She knew I was lonely. All those late nights."

"I know, old man. But even if you were the mark, how did she even know about Janet inheriting money?"

"It was that boyfriend of hers." He suddenly got angry. "She was a two-timing whore!" He spat out that last word. I looked up at Carter, who was grinning like he was watching the horse races and had the ticket to win on the longshot and it was coming around ahead of the pack by two lengths. It was infectious that smile. I started realizing the absolute absurdity of this entire conversation and how richly ironic the whole story was.

My father looked at me and then looked at Carter. The shadow of his real self suddenly showed up. "How dare you treat me that way, you... you... pansy!"

I looked up at Carter, who had his thick arms crossed, and said to my father, "That's a pansy? That's a fairy? Who do you think you're talking about?"

He spat at me. "I can't believe you have disgraced this family. You're just like that uncle of mine." He was beginning to either sober up or come to his senses, as appalling as they were.

I said, "This whole family is a disgrace. Janet was the one decent member. Remember how you used to beat her for taking bread to the men on California Street?"

He looked at me, now feeling some powerful emotion. At first, I thought he was going to cry again. But his real self was asserting and that show was over. "Those men were weak. They could have had any job they wanted."

"No, Father, there were no jobs to be had."

"Well, we can't run a charity for any slob down on his luck."

"Well, old man, Janet got you back for that." I briefly explained her trust and the will. I omitted any mention of the letters.

"The whole thing goes to your pansy Foundation?"

"Yes. It does."

He puffed up. "I'll sue!"

I shook my head. "I'm sure your white-shoe attorneys will be happy to take your money but I doubt the California State Supreme Court will be happy to see your bony ass back in front of them again. They already told you to take a hike once. Besides, you're loaded! What do you want more money for?"

He dropped his head, which was shocking. "All I've got is what's under the floor. And I've been selling off land. I'm not rich. Not anymore."

This knocked me back. I got up off my haunches and sat down in the chair next to him.

"Well, if you still have the mountain, you could live like a king and not have to worry about anything."

He looked at me, confused. "The mountain? What mountain?"

"That's the name Janet and I used to call that stash under your office."

He cracked the tiniest of smiles and then hid it, fast.

"No. There's not much there anymore. Only about a million."

Carter burst into laughter at this. I looked up at him and smiled. He covered his mouth quickly and then coughed.

My father looked up at Carter and said, "Don't laugh at me, young man. You may be big but you don't know what it's like to lose everything."

Carter said, "You must not have read today's paper, Dr. Williams."

My father turned to me and asked, "What is he talking about?"

I said, "First, he is a person. His name is Carter Jones and I love him."

My father shuddered. "Keep all that pansy stuff to yourself."

I pulled on my father's arm and said, "All that *pansy stuff* is on the front page of all the papers this morning."

"Except the *Examiner*," added Carter.

"What's that about the *Examiner*?" asked my father, looking at Carter and expecting an answer. I almost fell out of my chair.

"Your son, the genius, told off Mr. George Hearst in no uncertain terms last night when we were having dinner at the Top of the Mark."

My father turned to me and looked... proud? I wasn't sure what his look was, since I'd never seen it before. "You did?" He cracked the tiniest of smiles.

I nodded. He looked back up at Carter. "Well, boy, tell me what he said."

Carter looked mildly surprised and then gave a brief description, with lots of emphasis on my use of the word "rag."

My father, the evil old man that he was, actually cackled at one point. He looked at me, now smiling, and said, "Well, good for you."

I said, "Carter left out why I called him out."

He looked at me and said, "Oh, who cares? George Hearst is a pompous ass and I don't care why you did it. All that matters is that he was humiliated in public." He cackled again.

I stood up. "Well, it looks like you're back to your

usual evil self, so I guess we'll go in and have ourselves a memorial service if you're so disposed."

He shook his white head. "No. I'm going to stay in here until it's over. Then I'll go home. Do you think your giant friend will stay and keep me company?"

I really did almost fall over at this. I looked up at Carter. "Well, *friend*?"

He shrugged. "I'll stay here with you, Dr. Williams. But you have to cut out all that pansy crap. Otherwise, I'll throw you over my shoulder, take you outside, and show you what pansy actually means."

My father stood up and said, "Thank God someone in this family has a backbone."

I walked out of the room, stunned, and left the two of them in there.

. . .

The cathedral was still mostly packed. I walked the lonely trip up the aisle and resumed my seat. I nodded at the bishop, who then led us through a beautiful and touching service.

When it was over, I walked to the back and, flanked by Ben and Carlo, Mike, Pam and Diane, shook hands with everyone who wanted to stop and give their condolences, and many of them were very kind and generous.

Most everyone, however, had gotten what they came for and had rushed out to go sit at tea and gossip about the rotten Williams clan—the daughter who died young, the son who was a known homosexual, and the father who was a raving drunk. The gossip machines on Nob Hill would have plenty of fuel for weeks to come.

When it was all over, the bishop came to us and spoke some soothing words. He pulled me aside and asked about my father. "Believe it or not, Bishop, I left

Carter in that room with him, at his request."

The bishop's eyebrows went up. "Well, will miracles never cease?" I laughed.

I invited our little group to go for a stroll down California Street to Grant for some dim sum. Diane and Pam begged off because Diane wasn't sure they didn't still use dogs for meat in Chinatown. When we tried to persuade her otherwise, Pam intervened and said she had things to do at the house anyway, but thanks very much.

The guys, however, were in on the plan. I went to go find Carter, but the room was empty. I walked back over to the group and shrugged. We went outside in the blinding light of the beautiful day and found Carter standing on the steps talking to the reporter from the *Chronicle* who had given me the thumbs up the night before.

We gathered around just as Carter was saying, "It's going to be a kind of service never really available in one place before." I noticed the reporter was not really writing down much. He seemed to be very interested in Carter, however.

Mike stepped forward and handed the reporter a card. "Call me on Monday, and I'll give you all the information you want. Right now, we have a very important lunch meeting in Chinatown."

The reporter turned to him and asked, "And you are?"

"Michael Robertson, President of Consolidated Security."

I looked at him quizzically. He handed me a card. It said:

> Consolidated Security
> Nicholas Williams, C.E.O.
> Michael Robertson, President
> Marnie Wilson, Secretary
> 777 Bush Street
> San Francisco 8
> PRospect-7777

This was a pleasant surprise. I assumed that's what he'd been up to that morning. On a Saturday, no less.

The reporter lifted his hat to Mike and said, "Sure thing. I'll probably do a teaser in tomorrow's paper." He looked around and said, "Hey! Weren't all of you fired last night by the mayor?"

Mike nodded. "That's old news." He pointed at the card he'd handed the reporter. "This is the future."

The reporter looked at all of us. "You guys are my heroes."

Mike was all business. He said, "What we are is hungry. Call me at the number. Leave a message with the service if no one answers. I'll call you back. We'll get you a great story on the future of private security."

The reporter nodded and then ran down the steps.

We all walked down towards California Street together. This was the future. And, just like the day, it was looking bright indeed.

Author's Note

Thank you for buying and reading this book!

I hope you enjoyed this introduction to the world of Nick Williams and Carter Jones.

As I mention above in my Author's Introduction, when I first wrote this book, I didn't completely understand what it would develop into. As of this writing, I've completed sixteen additional books and feel like I've only barely scraped the surface of what is possible.

The proposition of this ongoing story is simple: what happens when someone is outed (long before that term was invented) and doesn't back down? Sure, Nick has nearly endless financial resources, but, as we discover in future books, the law isn't on his side and won't be for many years to come. How does this affect his friends and family? Will he always be able to buy himself out of every scrape? If you'd like to know more, *The Amorous Attorney* is next in line...

Acknowledgments

The details of this particular story came out of thin air. But the mood and the style of the tale is the evolution of a story that I had in mind for many years: a gay satire of the Perry Mason novels by Erle Stanley Gardner. His books have been favorites for many years. The gay twist was inspired by Mabel Maney's three novels featuring the lesbian adventures of Cherry Aimless, Nancy Clue, and their pals The Hardly Boys. They are great fun to read and I highly recommend them all.

J. B. Sanders, author of the Glen & Tyler series of books, is a personal hero who has written bold gay male characters in love. I want to acknowledge and thank him for all the hours of fun in reading his stories and for the inspiration his work has given me. I feel that, in a way that I hope pays homage where it is due, Nick & Carter are earlier, grittier versions of his protagonists.

For historical perspective and details, I have relied heavily on one particular book: *Wide-Open Town: A History of Queer San Francisco to 1965* by Nan Alamilla Boyd. I have referred to Ms. Boyd's research for the names of bars and nightclubs and specific historical events that affected the LGBT community of San Francisco. I have also relied on her descriptions of the era, which have been very useful. I am deeply grateful for her research and this book. Any mistakes, of course, are mine alone.

As to the form of writing a mystery, my chief inspiration is more from Dorothy L. Sayers than anyone else, although you may be hard-pressed to see that. If you know the Lord Peter mysteries, however, you may find a few small homages to them in these pages.

I was inspired to just sit down and write this first book after a number of helpful and powerful conversations with several friends: Benny, Paula, and Piper Jackson; Jody Ben-David, Edward Vilga, and Karen Cuccioli.

David Tangredi offered wonderful feedback and helped me remember that not everyone in the world watches old movies constantly. My favorite thing that he asked was, "Who is Winchell?"

Many thanks to everyone who has read, reviewed, and emailed me about the Nick & Carter books. It is deeply gratifying in ways that words will never be able to fully express. Thank you.

Finally, my mother, Carol Haggard, gave me the gift of storytelling or, at least, a deep interest in telling good stories. Hopefully that is what has happened here.

Added September 16, 2017: Many thanks to T.L., a loyal and devoted reader, who graciously informed me that Grace Cathedral in 1953 was still in a work in progress. He also gave me the forms of address for the Bishop of California. I've finally made those updates in this version and am deeply grateful for his help on this and many other topics.

Historical Notes

The events in this book take place between Monday, May 11, 1953, and Saturday, May 16, 1953.

The primary characters are all fictional. There are, however, several historical persons portrayed in a fictional manner.

Eddie Mannix was the infamous fixer who worked for Metro-Goldwyn-Mayer. He was recently portrayed by Josh Brolin in the Coen Brothers' movie, *Hail, Ceasar!* I first heard of Mr. Mannix through the most excellent podcast *You Must Remember This*, written and narrated by Karina Longworth. Neither Ms. Longworth nor Messrs. Coen has any responsibility for my particular portrayal of Mannix. His mistress and his wife's relationship with George Reeves, apparently with the consent of Mannix, are generally well-known.

George Hearst was the oldest son of newspaper magnate William Randolph Hearst. His youngest sibling was Randolph Hearst, now most famously known for being the father of Patricia. *The San Francisco Examiner* was called, "The Monarch of the Dailies," and was known to be the flagship publication of the Hearst Corporation.

In 1953, there were four newspapers published daily and distributed throughout the City: *The San Francisco Examiner*, *The San Francisco Chronicle*, *The San Francisco News*, and *The San Francisco Call-Bulletin*. There was a fierce rivalry between the four newspapers, so the idea of individuals rooting for one paper or despising another is very much in keeping with the times. The use of sordid headlines and the publishing of the names, addresses, and employers of men arrested during raids on gay bars during this period has been documented extensively. This happened in newspapers all over the United States. I borrowed the phrase, "Homo Nest Raided," from the *New York Daily News*, which used that phrase in its headline for the July 6, 1969 story that it published following the riots at the Stonewall Inn in June of 1969. My depiction of George Hearst is completely fictional although consistent to the time period.

San Francisco Mayor Elmer Edwin "Rob-Rob" Robinson was in office from 1948 through 1956.

Most of the locations referenced are correct, as far as I could verify. I consulted *Polk's San Francisco City Directory* for 1953 to verify business names and addresses. There is, however, no building at 777 Bush Street in the Tenderloin nor is there an unassuming bungalow at 137 Hartford Street in Eureka Valley. I verified both through the City & County of San Francisco Office of the Assessor-Recorder using their online property search database.

Eureka Valley is a neighborhood name that some readers may not recognize. It is the older name for the area now commonly referred to generally as The

Castro.

The Shell Building stands today, in all its understated glory, at the corner of Bush and Battery. According to Polk's, in 1953, the 10th floor was occupied by a division of Royal Dutch Shell, which was the primary tenant of the building until the 1960s.

One anachronism that eagle-eyed readers will immediately see is the use of the 4-digit local telephone number. PRospect-7777 would not have existed in 1953, as Pacific Telephone had already migrated to the 5-digit number for their exchanges in San Francisco to allow for long distance direct dialing. I did this on purpose so that I wouldn't have to use KLondike 5 as the exchange for all the phone numbers, not wanting to inadvertently use a current phone number.

One final thing: Owning or driving a 1953 Buick Skylark is now on my bucket list! That looks like one sweet ride!

Credits

Yesteryear Font (headings) used with permission under SIL Open Font License, Version 1.1. Copyright © 2011 by Brian J. Bonislawsky DBA Astigmatic (AOETI). All rights reserved.

Gentium Book Basic Font (body text) used with permission under the SIL Open Font License, Version 1.1. Copyright © 2002 by J. Victor Gaultney. All rights reserved.

Gladifilthefte Font (cover) by Tup Wanders used under a Creative Commons license by attribution.

Langdon Font (cover) provided freely by XLN Telecom.

My Underwood Font (telegrams) used with permission. Copyright © 2009 by Tension Type. All rights reserved.

Cover photo of woman by Chris Lund used via Creative Commons (CC BY 2.0). Photo digitized by Library and Archives Canada (e010949002).

More Information

Be the first to know about new releases:

frankwbutterfield.com

Printed in Great Britain
by Amazon